ISBN 978-1-331-81453-5
PIBN 10238227

English
Français
Deutsche
Italiano
Español
Português

www.forgottenbooks.com

Mythology Photography **Fiction**
Fishing Christianity **Art** Cooking
Essays Buddhism Freemasonry
Medicine **Biology** Music **Ancient**
Egypt Evolution Carpentry Physics
Dance Geology **Mathematics** Fitness
Shakespeare **Folklore** Yoga Marketing
Confidence Immortality Biographies
Poetry **Psychology** Witchcraft
Electronics Chemistry History **Law**
Accounting **Philosophy** Anthropology
Alchemy Drama Quantum Mechanics
Atheism Sexual Health **Ancient History**
Entrepreneurship Languages Sport
Paleontology Needlework Islam
Metaphysics Investment Archaeology
Parenting Statistics Criminology
Motivational

THE LIFE OF ADMIRAL KEPPEL.

By the HON. and REV. THOMAS KEPPEL.

In 2 vols., 8vo., with Portrait.

" 'I ever looked on Lord Keppel,' says Edmund Burke, ' as one of the greatest and best men of his age, and I loved and cultivated him accordingly; he was much in my heart, and I believe I was in his to the very last beat.' This first authentic memoir, rich in matters of lively and various interest, by his kinsman, supplies a blank in that glorious portion of our English annals so recently enriched with the lives of Anson, Rodney, and Howe; of the first of whom Keppel was the pupil, of the second the friend, and of the last the companion in arms."—*Examiner.*

THE EARL OF MUNSTER'S MEMOIRS. OF THE LATE WAR.

To which is added the Personal Narrative of Captain Cooke of the 43rd Regiment, containing new particulars of the Battles of Salamanca, Vittoria, Pampeluna, Nivelle, Toulouse, and of the Sieges of Ciudad Rodrigo, Badajoz, and St. Sebastian.

2 vols., small 8vo., 21s.
" A volume full of interest."—*Quarterly Review.*

LIEUT.-COL. NAPIER'S LETTERS FROM
THE SHORES OF THE MEDITERRANEAN.

2 vols. small 8vo., 21s. bound.

" These volumes comprise a fund of entertainment and information, full of life, spirit, and reality, and affording one of the pleasantest pictures of the life of a soldier and a traveller united in one, that can any where he met with."—*Naval and Military Gazette.*

MAJOR-GENERAL SIR CHAS. NAPIER'S
" LIGHTS AND SHADES OF MILITARY LIFE."

2 vols. small 8vo., 21s. bound.

" Two of the most agreeable volumes we have for a long time met with. They are replete with every charm of novelty."—*Morning Herald.*

CAPT. D. H. O'BRIEN'S ADVENTURES
DURING THE LATE WAR,

Comprising a Narrative of Shipwreck, Captivity, Escapes from French Prisons, &c., from 1804 to 1827.

2 vols. 8vo., with illustrations, 28s. bound.

THE

LIGHT DRAGOON.

BY THE AUTHOR OF

" THE SUBALTERN," " CHELSEA PENSIONERS,"
" THE HUSSAR," &c.

IN TWO VOLUMES.

VOL. I.

LONDON:

HENRY COLBURN, PUBLISHER,
GREAT MARLBOROUGH STREET.

———

1844.

C. WHITING, BEAUFORT HOUSE, STRAND.

ADVERTISEMENT.

THE following pages come before the Public, under circumstances which will, I trust, be accepted as a sufficient apology for their appearance as a separate work.

About four years ago, the hero of the narrative, George Farmer, formerly a private in the 11th Light Dragoons, came to me to complain, as many of his class are accustomed to do, of poverty. He told me, at the same time, that he had kept a journal of his proceedings during more than twenty years of a somewhat eventful life; and begged that I would take the trouble to read, and if possible, turn it for him to some account. I accordingly read his story. It seemed to me sufficiently interesting to warrant its insertion, as a series of papers, in a professional magazine; and with this view I rewrote the narrative and sent it to Mr. Colburn.

Mr. Colburn has remunerated the old soldier to his heart's content, and more than compensated me for the trouble which I have had. He has likewise come to the conclusion, that the tale is not unworthy to be collected into the form which it has now assumed; and I shall be very glad to find that he is no loser by his liberality.

G. R. G.

Chelsea College,
Nov. 1843.

THE

LIGHT DRAGOON.

CHAPTER I.

How I enlisted, and what befel me then.

As I cannot imagine that among such as
may honour these pages by a perusal, there
are any who would take much interest in the
personal history of one so humble as myself, I think it best to pass over all the
incidents of my early life, and to come at
once to the period of my enlistment. Who
I am, where I was born, to what class of
society my father and mother belonged, are

points with which I alone am concerned. And for the rest, it is fair to avow, that if the incidents of my boyhood were all strung together, they would not make up a tale worth telling, far less a . narrative which would for a single hour be remembered.

I entered the service in the summer of 1808, by enlisting as a private in the 11th regiment of Light Dragoons. The corps being at that time stationed in Ireland, I was sent with several recruits besides, to the depot at Maidstone; where for some time I ran the career which is appointed for recruits in general, and acquired some knowledge of the darker shades in human nature, if I learned nothing better. It unfortunately happens, however, that our first experience of this great book is not often favourable to our morals; and I confess that I am not an exception to the general rule. My extreme youth—for I was not more than seventeen years of age—exposed me to many and great temptations. The same circumstance laid me open to chicanery and deceit on the part of those around me; and I lament to say, that I became the victim as well of my own folly as of the knavery of others. How I suffered from the former of these evils, it is not worth while to tell. Young men would scarce take the trouble to follow my details, were I to give them; and if they did, I am quite sure they would never condescend to be warned by them. But it is not impossible that they may think it worth while to attend to such of my admonitions as seem to bear upon the behaviour of others; and I accordingly request that they will take good heed of the following aphorisms:

1. When you join your depot, you usually arrive with a good deal of money in your pocket; that is to say, you get your bounty as soon as you have passed, and appear in your own eyes to be enormously rich. Be assured that it is quite possible ·

to run through as much as ten or twelve guineas: and don't take the trouble to throw your shillings and halfcrowns at people's heads, as if they were of no value.

2· You find a comrade particularly civil: begin to suspect he has fallen in love—not with you, but your money; and button up your pockets in exact proportion to the zeal which he manifests for trying their depth.

3. Non-commissioned officers are in an especial manner to be shunned, whenever they profess to hold you in favour, or seem to relax the bonds of discipline, in order that you may not be distressed by them. These harpies desire only to make a prey of you. They will first suck you dry, and then grind you to powder. .

4. Endeavour to begin your career as it is your wisdom not less than your duty to go forward with it. Aim at the character of a sober and steady man, and you will, without doubt, succeed in deserving it.

5. Keep your temper, even if you be wronged, especially when the wrong is put upon you by a superior. Truth and justice are sure to prevail in the end; whereas, it often happens that he who is eager to anticipate that end is crushed in the struggle.

6. Finally, be alert in striving to acquire all necessary drills, and an acquaintance with your duty in general. It will be of far more benefit to you to be well thought of by a few good men, and by your officers, than to to be called "a capital fellow" by scores of scamps, who will only laugh at your remorse so soon as they have succeeded in bringing you into trouble.

But I am fast getting into a prose, so let me pull up; otherwise I may fail to carry, as I intend to do, public interest along with me.

Well, then, I enlisted in London; and, marching to Maidstone, underwent the customary examinations; after which I was attested before a magistrate, and had my bounty paid with strict exactitude. Unfortunately for me, however, the society into which I was thrown bore no resemblance at all to a well-regulated regiment. The barracks were filled with small detachments from a countless variety of corps, and the sergeants and corporals, on whom the internal discipline both of regiments and depots mainly depends, seem to me, at this distance of time, to have been selected from the very scum of the earth. Like a band of harpies, they pounced upon us recruits, and never let us loose from their talons till they had thoroughly pigeoned us. We were invited to their rooms of an evening,—introduced to their wives, who made much of us,— praised, favoured, screened, and cajoled, till our funds began to run low, and then they would have nothing more to say to us. Under these circumstances, we were sufficiently well pleased when the order came to join the regiment at Clonmel: and, being put in charge of one Corporal Gorman, we began our journey, profoundly ignorant both of the route we were to follow, and the extent of funds which would be allowed us during the continuance of the march.

An admirable specimen was Corporal Gorman of the sort of land-sharks out . of which the staff of the recruiting department used long ago to be formed. His first step was to extract from each of us, in the shape of a loan, whatever happened to remain of our bounty. His next, to defraud us of the better half of our marching-money, by paying over to us, respectively, day by day, one shilling, and applying one shilling and a· penny to his own use. Like bad men in general, however, whom long impunity has hardened, he committed the mistake, in the end, of overshooting his mark, and we having been much irritated by his tyrannical behaviour, reported him, when at Lichfield, to a magistrate. It appeared that he was not now about to form his first acquaintance with that functionary. His worship knew him well; and, by a threat of bringing the case before the general commanding the district, soon forced the knave to pay back the money which we, in our simplicity, had lent him. The arrears of our marching-money on the other hand, we never succeeded in recovering. He promised, indeed, from stage to stage, that all should be cleared off; and prevailed upon us, on our arrival in Dublin, to sign our accounts, which he himself had made up, and by which we acknowledged that we had been fully settled with. But he entirely forgot to return, as he had pledged himself to do, the sum that was needed to render the acknowledgment accurate; and, quietly handing us over to a worthy not unlike himself, took his passage in the packet for Holyhead, and left us.

I joined the head-quarters of my regiment

at Clonmel at a moment when both town and country rang with the exploits of two celebrated robbers, called, respectively, Brennan and Hogan. Brennan, as all the world knows, was originally a soldier—unless my memory be at fault—in the 12th Light Dragoons; from which regiment he deserted in consequence of some quarrel with one of the officers, that he might take, after the fashion of Dick Turpin of old, to the road. His courage was as reckless as his presence of mind was astonishing; neither of which, however, would have much availed, had he not, at the same time, been thoroughly acquainted with the *locale* of the scene of his operations; but in this respect his advantages were fully as remarkable as in others, for there was not a hole or crevice in the counties of Cork, Tipperary, and Wexford, with which he seems not to have been familiar. Moreover, Brennan displayed, in the management of his reckless business, quite as much of sound policy as of hardihood. He was never known to rob, or in any way to molest, a peasant, an artisan, or a small farmer. He made war, and professed to make war only upon the rich, out of the plunder taken from whom he would often assist the poor; and the poor in return not only refused to betray him, but took care that he should be warned in time, whenever any imminent danger seemed to threaten. The consequence was, that for full five years—a long space of time for a highwayman to be at large, even in Ireland—he continued to levy contributions upon all who came in his way, and had always about him the means of satisfying his own wishes. As might be expected, a great clamour was raised. Government was petitioned for troops wherewith to hunt him down. Large rewards were offered to any persons who should betray him: and day and night the magistracy of the counties were abroad, with dragoons at their heels, striving to intercept him. I heard that on one occasion, when Lord Caher, the most indefatigable of his pursuers, ran him hard, his horse became spent ere it could carry him to the Kilworth hill; and that it was only by quitting the saddle, and diving into the recesses of a wood, close by, that he managed to make good his escape. His favourite roadster fell, on that occasion, into the hands of his enemies; and he never ceased to lament the circumstance as a very grievous calamity.

Of Hogan I am unable to say more than that common report spoke of him as a pedler, whose brave resistance to Brennan's attack originally won for him the friendship of the outlaw. It is said that the bandit fell in with his future associate one day when the pressure of want was peculiarly severe upon him. He had alighted, for some purpose or another, when the pedler came up; and, not anticipating any resistance, he carelessly desired the latter to render up his pack. But the pedler, instead of obeying the command, closed instantly with his assailant. A fierce struggle took place between them, neither having time to appeal to the deadly weapons with which both, it appeared, were armed.

" Who the devil are you?" said Brennan at last, after he had rolled with his antagonist in the dust till both were weary. " Sure, then, I didn't think there was a man in all Tipperary as could have fought so long with Bill Brennan."

" Och, then, blood and ouns !" exclaimed the other, "if you be Brennan, arrah! then, arn't I Paddy Hogan ? and if you cry stand to all the world in Tipperary, sure don't I do that same to the folks in Cork?"

This was quite enough for Brennan. He entertained too high a respect for his own profession to exercise it in hostility towards a brother of the order; so he struck up, on the instant, an alliance with the pedler, and the two thenceforth played one into the hands of the other.

Of the manner in which Brennan was accustomed to do his work, the following anecdote will give a just idea:

Once upon a time, when the regiment of —— Militia lay in quarters at Clonmel, two of the officers drove, in a one-horse chaise, to Fethard, where they had engaged to be present at a public dinner that was to be eaten at the principal inn in the place. They joined the company as they had proposed to do, and sat till a late hour at night, when, their companions departing, they likewise ordered their gig, and walked into what was called the travellers'-room till it should be brought round to the door. There were several strangers in the room; one of whom, a well-dressed man, stood by the fire. But of these the militia officers took no notice, their heads, as it appeared, being filled with anticipations of what might befal on their way back to Clonmel. One, indeed, did not hesitate to express regret that they had sat so late.

" These are troublesome times," observed he; "and who knows but we may encounter Brennan himself?"

" What of that?" was the answer. " You and I are surely not afraid to encounter one man. We have a brace of pistols: only let the scoundrel show himself, and see how I'll handle him!"

The stranger who lounged over the fire looked up as these words were uttered, but took no notice of them. Only, when they quitted the apartment he withdrew also,—no salutation or mark of courtesy having passed between them.

The gig being by this time brought round, the two militia officers took their seats, and in high goodhumour and excellent spirits drove off. They continued their journey for a while without meeting with any adventure; till all at once, just as they had reached a peculiarly dismal part of the road, a man sprang from one of the ditches, and seized the horse's head.

"I'll trouble you, gentlemen," said he, presenting a pistol towards them at the same time, "to alight. I should be very sorry to hurt either of you; but by my soul! if you don't do as I bid you, or try to open the locker, I'll blow your brains out in a jiffy. It shall be no joke to you, anyhow."

The officers sat stock-still, staring at each other, and not knowing what to make of it; but at last one, less flabbergasted than the other, exclaimed—

" And who the devil are you, that we should accommodate you in that manner?"

" Gentlemen," was the reply, " my name is Brennan."

There was magic in the sound of the word. Not another question was put, not another remonstrance offered, but, making all possible haste, both of them sprang to the ground, and stood as if waiting the bandit's further orders. Brennan, however, was by no means a sanguinary person; and in the present instance he had a whim to indulge as well as a booty to collect. He instantly assumed the vacated seat, and gathering up the reins, looked down upon his discomfited foes, and cried, " The next time you happen to make mention of my name, you'll probably treat it with more respect." So saying, he wheeled round, and wishing the militia-men good night, drove off.

A comfortless tramp these heroes had of it, over a dozen miles of muddy road, ere they reached Clonmel. They slunk quietly to their barrack-rooms, however, being extremely desirous of concealing their own shame, and Brennan's triumph from the knowledge of their brother-officers; and for a space of not less than six months they succeeded. But at the termination of that period, when the regiment stood under arms at evening parade, a boy entered the barrack-yard, leading in his hand a horse and gig, both of which were familiar to every one present. The boy walked up to the commanding officer and handed him a note, which he read with evident astonishment. This, of course, increased the curiosity of the rest, who gathered round their colonel, while our two chap-fallen heroes slank away, and took refuge in their own quarters. The colonel was desired to read aloud. He did so ; and then the boy being questioned, the whole secret came out. Amid shouts of laughter from the audience to which he addressed himself, the urchin imitated Brennan's style of telling the story, and then, not without some substantial marks of the officer's favour, he was permitted to withdraw. It is scarcely necessary to add, that the two worthies who, carrying arms, forgot at the moment of trial, to make use of them, never showed themselves again in the ranks of the —— militia.

Brennan's career, though a very remarkable one, could scarce, in the nature of things, terminate otherwise than in his own destruction. Many a narrow escape he made, many a feat of daring and activity he performed; but in the end, accident proved more fatal to him than all the designs and projects of his pursuers. It happened, one day, that a gentleman riding along the high-road, observed two men creep through a gap in one of the hedges, and disappear on the other side. He instantly conceived the notion that they might be Brennan and his ally, the pedler; so he hurried off to Lord Caher, and told both what he knew and what he conjectured. His lordship's eagerness to effect the capture of the bandit had not abated a jot, and, thinking it highly probable that his informant's suspicion might be well founded, he gave orders for a detachment of the 11th to mount their horses, and directed, at the same time, the Sligo militia to march with all haste, and extending their files to surround the spot. . For within this hedge, through which the mysterious strangers had been seen to pass, was a new house, as yet incomplete, with a stack or two of furze cut down and piled up for fuel; and his lordship justly concluded, that if he could make of these the centre of a circle, of which the radii should be respectively half a mile in length, he might pretty surely count on picking up every living thing that might have established itself, either by accident or design, within the circumference of that circle.

I well remember that I formed one of the mounted detachment, which performed the service of which I am now speaking, and the strange excitement of the chase, I shall never, till my dying day, forget. The militia marched as they were directed, and, extending their files, soon placed the unfinished domicile, with its appurtenances, within a cordon. This was gradually narrowed, while our mounted men kept a lookout in the rear, and made ready to start off in desperate pursuit, should the game be sprung, and trust to speed of foot for escape. By-and-by the infantry closed upon the house, searched it through, and found it empty; it may be imagined there was an expression of blank astonishment in every face, till one of our men suddenly exclaimed, "You haven't examined the chimney; you may depend upon it you'll find him there." It was no sooner said than done; for the speaker sprang from his horse, ran inside, poked his head up the kitchen chimney, and in an instant withdrew it again. It was well for him that he did so, for almost simultaneously with his backward leap, came the report of a pistol, the ball from which struck the hearth without wounding any body. It is impossible for me to describe the scene that followed. Nobody cared to get below the robber; nobody fancied that it would be possible to get above him; and threats and smooth speeches were soon shown to be alike unavailing to draw him from his hiding-place. But the marvel of the adventure did not stop there. While a crowd of us were gathered about the house, some shouting on Brennan to surrender, others firing at the top of the chimney, a sort of salute which the robber did not hesitate to answer,—one of the Sligo men suddenly called out from the rear, that he had pricked a man with his bayonet among the gorse. In an instant search was made, and sure enough there lay Brennan himself, on his back in a narrow ditch, with a brace of pistols close beside his feet, of which, however, he did not judge it expedient to make use. He was instantly seized, disarmed, and put in charge of a sufficient guard; while the remainder of us addressed ourselves to the capture of his companion, concerning whom we could not for an instant doubt that he was Hogan.

When Brennan gave himself up, he did so with a singularly mild and serene aspect. There was no expression of ferocity in his countenance; no look which could be understood to imply either bitter agony because of the fate which had overtaken him, or a desperate resolution to sell his life at the highest. His whole bearing, on the contrary, was that of a man perfectly reconciled to his fate; not, indeed, very hopeful, yet far from desperate; and, therefore, little disposed to shed either his own or any other person's blood unnecessarily. Hogan, on the contrary, resembled one of the wild beasts, which in Norway, or some of the other countries where *battues* are carried on upon a scale more magnificent than in England, the hunters contrive to hem within their toils, seeking to capture him alive rather than kill him; for Hogan would not listen to any proposal of surrender. He mounted, on the contrary, to the very edge of the chimney, making of its brickwork a sort of parapet to protect him from our bullets, and fired pistol after pistol, till his ammunition became exhausted, and he was forced, with extreme reluctance, to descend. "In the name of common sense," said Lord Caher, "why did you offer such a useless resistance? you knew all the while that you must be taken at last—why then wantonly put your own and other men's lives in jeopardy?" But Hogan would not condescend to reply. He drew up his tall muscular figure to the utmost, and looking disdainfully upon the throng that surrounded him, he continued silent.

Brennan and Hogan were placed each on the croup of a horseman's saddle, and in this manner, under a sufficient escort, were conveyed to the watch-house in Caher. It seemed to me that Hogan evinced manifest tokens of satisfaction, as soon as he ascertained that he stood not alone in misfortune; a strange disposition, yet the reverse of uncommon, and indicative of no extraordinary ferocity on the part of him who is swayed by it. But however this may be, the prisoners rode on contentedly enough, and were in due time safely lodged in their narrow quarters.

It seemed, however, that neither the inconveniences attached to the cell, nor their anticipation of the fate that was before them, had any power to work mischievously upon their humour. How Hogan conducted himself I cannot so decidedly describe; but of Brennan, it is fresh in my recollection, that he was throughout singularly cheerful and confiding. He told us many stories of his own narrow escapes. He pointed out several of our men who had more than once been in pursuit of him, and whose lives, he declared, had

over and over again been in his hands, though
a sense of what was right would not permit
him to take them. "Why should I shoot
you?" was the tenour of his appeal. "I have
been a soldier in my day, and know that a
soldier must obey whatever orders he may
receive. No, no—I should have the guilt
of Cain on my soul, had any one of your
regiment died by my hands; and yet more
than once you had wellnigh forced me to
the extremity." Then he would launch out
in praise of his favourite mare, whose death
he deplored as the severest calamity that
ever befel him, and invariably wound up by
expressing his conviction, that after all he
would never be hanged. "There is no proof
against me," was his argument. "There's
nobody to swear that by me he was ever
wronged; and were the fact different, I am
sure that the people will not permit me to
be put to death." In this respect, however,
Brennan had deceived himself; for the law,

when it puts forth its might is, even in Ireland, stronger than the mere will or caprice of a mob.

Having been detained in the guard-room of Caher all night, the prisoners were removed next day to Clonmel, where, in due time, the assizes came on, and they were put upon their trial. Many charges were brought against both, and especially against Brennan; yet the robber was so far in the right, that nobody could be persuaded to swear to his identity. At length a quaker, whose carriage had been robbed near Fermoy, mounted the witness-box, and went so far as to declare a belief, that he saw in Brennan the individual who had stopped it. He would not, indeed, assert positively that the case was so,—he only believed that Brennan was the man. On this evidence, not very explicit we must allow, yet, without doubt the best which could, under the circumstances, be procured, Brennan was found guilty; and both he and Hogan, who, on some such evidence, was in like manner convicted, received sentence of death. How shall I describe the scene that followed? Multitudes from all parts of the surrounding country, and from the distance, in some instances, of fifty miles from the town, had flocked in to witness the trial; and now that their idol was doomed to die, their grief and consternation exceeded all conceivable bounds. Bearded men wept in the court-house like children. There were groans, deep and bitter, rising from every quarter; and more than one, especially among the women, fainted away, and was carried out. Meanwhile the troops, anticipating an attempt at rescue, stood to their arms, and the whole night long the streets were patroled; but no disturbance took place. After indulging for an hour or two in useless howling, the crowd melted away, and long before midnight a profound calm pervaded every corner of the town.

At last the terrible day of execution arrived, and Brennan, with his associate, being placed in an open cart, passed about half-past nine in the morning, under a strong military escort, beneath the arched gateway of the gaol. Again had formidable preparations been made to meet and repel violence, should any be offered: but again the thunder-cloud dispersed, without any outburst of its fury. The crowd, to be sure, was prodigious; but what can a mere crowd attempt or hope to accomplish against even a handful of disciplined and well-armed soldiers? and where, as happened to be the case that day, the soldiers are numerous, then must even the thought of resistance be scouted. Not a hand was raised in defence of the prisoners during all the progress from the prison to the gallows, and round the gallows the

multitudes that assembled stood, if not mute,
at all events motionless. It was curious at
the time to mark the difference of character
that showed itself in the bearings of the two
men: Brennan gazed cheerfully round him
all the while he was in the cart, and recognising in the crowd several of his friends,
perhaps followers, he nodded and smiled to
them gaily. Hogan, on the contrary, though
equally self-collected, was far more reserved,
for he never bestowed upon any of the
throng one mark of recognition, nor once
addressed a word to his fellow-sufferer. Yea,
and after the cords had been adjusted, and
the unhappy men stood, waiting for the
signal which should carry the vehicle from
beneath, and leave them to die between earth
and heaven;—even then Hogan turned aside
with undisguised contempt and loathing,
from the hand which his associate offered to
his pressure; and wrapping himself up in
his own thoughts, sternly and resolutely pre-

pared for the issue. It was not long of coming.
At a given signal the cart drove away, and
amid yells, more loud and terrible than men
ever utter, except in the Emerald Isle, the
souls of these two noted malefactors were
wrenched from their bodies. I must not,
however, forget to mention, that the two renowned highwaymen suffered not alone. A
young man, found guilty of forcibly carrying
away a girl from her home and the protection of her parents, was the same day exe-
cuted in pursuance of his sentence ; and he
chose to die in a garb which excited not
only our surprise, but our ridicule. He
came to be hanged in a garment of white
flannel, made tight to the shape, and ornamented in all directions with knots of blue
ribbon, rather more befitting a harlequin on
the stage, than a wretched culprit whose life
had become forfeit to the offended laws.

CHAPTER II.

Service in Ireland, and Embarkation for Portugal.

THROUGHOUT the whole period of my sojourn in Tipperary, amounting to not less than seven months, the peace of the county was disturbed, and men's lives put in continual jeopardy, by the prevalence of party feuds, far more desperate in their nature than any with which the present generation seems to be familiar. There were two factions in particular, the Shanavests and Caravats, who waged one upon the other an unceasing war of extermination. Every day brought to our quarters the report of some murder or horrid personal outrage—every night made known to us that some act of incendiarism had been perpetrated. Highway robbery, too, was very frequent, insomuch that the mail never passed from point to point, except under an escort of dragoons; while smuggling was carried on to such a degree, that the trade of the licensed distiller brought him no returns. A melancholy time of it had we under such circumstances. What with constant demands to protect a gentleman's house, or calls upon us to assist in extinguishing the flames that had been applied to it; what with escorts to protect the mail, parties to put down a still, patrols to keep the roads safe, and guards to preserve the peace at different fairs, neither we nor our horses knew what it was to have four-and-twenty hours on which we could count, as disposable for purposes—I do not say of relaxation, but—of ordinary regimental or common duty. Our entire life was one of alarms, excursions, and disappointments; for I cannot deny, that we became in the end extremely irritated towards the people whose misconduct thus harassed us; and, as a necessary consequence, were deeply mortified as often as we failed in. making prisoners of the wretches whose violations of the law broke in so often upon our repose.

Among the various painful duties, which then engaged me, there is not one on which I now look back with more unmixed abhorrence that the operation of still-hunting. There was no hour of the night or day at which we could consider ourselves free from the chance of being roused and sent forth, we knew not whither, under the guidance of an excise officer. Unless my memory mislead me, too, these demands upon our activity came with much greater frequency during the night than when the sun was shining; while winter seemed to be the season when the smuggler chiefly plied his trade, doubtless with the laudable desire of rendering

our researches among the mountains as little
agreeable to us as possible. How often have
I been roused from my warm bed, required
to saddle and mount my horse amid pitchy
darkness, and sent forth, I could not tell in
what direction, to achieve a conquest over
an iron pot and a tin worm! Ay, and what is
more, the conquest, contemptible as in the
ear of the civilian it may sound, was not
always achieved. It is marvellous with what
accuracy the distillers received information
of our movements—often when we flattered
ourselves that we were least open to the eye
of scrutiny. Over and over again, I have
ridden long miles through the mountain
passes, my horse floundering in the snow, or
tripping over pits and holes, to the imminent risk both of my neck and his own;
and after all, when we reached the spot
where the seizure was to have been effected,
we found nothing save the traces of an extinguished fire, and two or three peasants,

who never omitted to laugh at us. In like manner, the duties of escorting the mail were by no means agreeable. Amid thickets, or in the ditches, parties of armed men would lie, who would sometimes kill both men and horses with their fire, while for us to search for them, except through the medium of our carbines, was impossible.

It is not, however, because of these annoyances alone that my recollection of service in Ireland is any thing but agreeable to myself, or creditable to the temper of the people. I admit that provisions were cheap, that whiskey was abundant, and that I never saw an individual Irishman of a temper, which may not deserve to be described as generous, and hospitable, and open. But as a people they were perfect savages, not merely in their mode of dealing with those against whom they entertained a feud; but against persons in whose society they set out with professing to take delight, and with whom they got drunk in all the glee imaginable. The case, for example, was not unfrequent of a party coming in to a public-house to drink, carousing together in perfect goodhumour till their senses became confused, and then quarrelling vehemently, they could not tell why. Forthwith came into play, poker, shovel, tongs, benches, and knives, till many a time the floor of the tap-room swam with blood, and of the persons frequenting it not a few were borne off grievously, sometimes mortally, wounded. Then their fairs and wakes were invariably of such a nature, that troops were sent to observe them, and to hinder the commission of all manner of violence. Yet even this precaution was not invariably found to avail. I remember, for example, that not far from the town in which we were quartered, an event befell, of which even now it is not easy to write without a shudder. There had been a funeral, which, coming from some remote corner in the country, was attended by a score or two. of ragged peasants, all of whom followed the corpse, howling as is their wont, and nowise insensible to the stimulating influence of strong drink. The mourners having deposited their deceased friend in his grave, adjourned, as a matter of course, to the whiskey-shop, where they pledged his memory in as many draughts as the state of their finances would allow. Having exhausted these, and thoroughly inflamed themselves, they set out to return home; and well would it have been had they followed up this resolution, without looking either to the right hand or to the left.

The persons who carried the corpse to its grave, belonged to one or other of the rival factions, I cannot tell which. That, however, is a matter of no moment, for both were alike ferocious, and either would have been guilty in this particular instance of the horrible crimes of which I am about to make mention. Having drunk freely, as has been stated, the mourners set out to return home, and came, as they proceeded, upon the house of a respectable farmer, who owed allegiance to a party hostile to their own. Like madmen, they sprang within the inclosure, burst open his door, and meeting the servant girl in the passage, instantly put her to death. They then rushed into the kitchen, where the farmer and his wife were seated, an aged couple, from whom no molestation could be apprehended: them they pierced with many wounds; after which, they slew the cows in the stall, the horses in the stable, and the very dog and cat that wandered about the premises. In a word, a more atrocious massacre never was perpetrated, even in the county of Tipperary, though Tipperary has in all ages been renowned for the little value which its inhabitants put either upon their own lives, or on the lives of other people.

After this account of the duties which were imposed upon us, and the sort of life which we led while quartered at Clonmel, it will scarcely be wondered at when I say that the order which one day reached us, to march forthwith upon Dublin, was by me greeted with unqualified satisfaction. The 23rd light dragoons having been directed to proceed on foreign service, it became our business to supply their place; and this we did early in the spring of 1809, our respective squadrons meeting, on more than one occasion, as they moved,—we to the capital, they towards Cork harbour. We occupied Dublin for something more than a year; and had the satisfaction, such as it was, of witnessing there the celebration of the great Jubilee. I need scarcely add, that the Jubilee of which I speak commemorated the fiftieth year of the reign of

George III., and was kept up with extraordinary spirit in all parts of his majesty's dominions. I greatly question, however, whether in any town throughout the empire, more of the external show of loyalty was exhibited than in Dublin. For three whole days men exhibited their gladness, first by a grand review of the troops in St. Stephen's ·Green; next by a general illumination; and last of all in a sort of carnival, where all manner of irregularities were freely perpetrated, no human being caring to find fault with them. For example, the streets were thronged both night and day with minstrels, maskers, and mummers; for whom every door was thrown freely open, and who were regaled wherever they came with vivres and a hearty welcome. Neither, as far as I know, was any advantage taken of such frankness to work evil to the persons or the property of the individuals who displayed it. Yet we had slender reason to congratulate ourselves that we happened to be present on so animating an occasion: from four o'clock in the afternoon of one day, till seven in the following morning, both we and the Scots Greys were employed to patrol the streets; one half of the town being intrusted to the care of the Greys, and the other committed to our especial keeping. We all did our duty, without doubt; yet we heartily rejoiced when the gaieties came to an end, and we were permitted to return to the ordinary occupation of our lives.

So passed the year 1809, of which my general recollections amount to this, and no more—that if not positively an era in my existence, it has left no stamp of extreme misery on my soul. Still there was very little mourning in the corps when the arrival of the 7th Hussars set us free, and we embarked, in the same transports which brought them into the Liffey, for Holyhead. There we landed in safety: a pleasant march of twenty-two days carried us to Weymouth, where the head-quarters of the regiment being established, detachments went abroad to various out-stations, of which Farnham and Porchester were two. At the latter of these posts I found myself, with twenty of my comrades, the charge being committed to us of keeping guard over French prisoners, who, to the number of 7000 at the least, were cooped up within the walls of the castle.

Whatever grounds of boasting may belong to us as a nation—and I am the last man in the world to think of diminishing their number, I am afraid that our mode of dealing with the prisoners taken from the French during the war scarcely deserves to be classed among them. Absolute cruelties were never, I believe, perpetrated on those unfortunate beings; neither, as far as I know, were they, on any pretence whatever, stinted in the allowance of food awarded to them. But, in other respects they fared hardly enough. Their sleeping apartments, for instance, were very much crowded. Few paroles were extended to them, (it is past dispute, that when the parole was obtained, they were, without distinction of rank, apt to make a bad use of it,) while their pay was calculated on a scale as near to the line of starvation, as could in any measure correspond with our national renown for humanity. On the other hand, every possible encouragement was given to the exercise of ingenuity among the prisoners themselves, by the throwing open of the castle yard once or twice a week, when their wares were exhibited for sale, amid numerous groups of jugglers, tumblers, and musicians, all of whom followed their respective callings, if not invariably with skill, always with most praiseworthy perseverance.

Moreover, the ingenuity of the captives, taught them how, on these occasions, to set up stalls, on which all manner of trinkets were set forth, as well as puppet-shows, and Punch's opera,—in witnessing which, John Bull's good humour was sure to be called into play. Then followed numerous purchases, particularly on the part of the country people, of bone and ivory nicknacks, fabricated invariably with a common penknife, yet always neat and not unfrequently elegant. Nor must I forget to mention the daily market, which the peasantry, particularly the women, were in the habit of attending, and which usually gave scope for the exchange of Jean Crapaud's manufactures for Nancy's eggs, or Joan's milk, or home-baked loaf. This, though it took place at an early hour in the morning, was day after day an interesting spectacle to us, who, not seeking to pry beyond the mere surface of things, were apt to quit the castle-yard with a notion, that, after all, the prisoners had no great cause to be dissatisfied with their lot.

A prisoner, however, is always dissatisfied with his lot—how indeed can he be otherwise? and we at Porchester, like others employed on a similar duty elsewhere, were in due time taught the truth of this axiom. It happened one night, that a sentry, whose post lay outside the walls of the old castle, was startled by a sound as of a hammer driven against the earth beneath his feet. The man stopped, listened, and was more and more convinced, that neither his fears nor his imagination had misled him; so he reported the circumstance to the serjeant, who next visited his post, and left him to take in the matter such steps as might be expedient. The serjeant, as in duty bound, having first ascertained that the man spoke truly, made his report to the captain on duty, who immediately doubled the sentry at the indicated spot, and gave strict orders, that should so much as one French prisoner be seen making his way beyond the castle walls, he should be shot without mercy. Then was the whole of the guard got under arms; then were beacons fired in various quarters, while far and near, from Portsmouth not less than from the cantonments, more close at hand, bodies of troops marched upon Porchester. Among others came the general of the district, bringing with him a detachment of sappers and miners; by whom all the floors of the several bed-rooms were tried, and who soon brought the matter home to those engaged in it. Indeed, one man at last was taken in the gallery which he was seeking to enlarge; his only instrument being a spike nail wherewith to labour.

The plot thus detected was a very extensive, and must, if carried through, have proved a desperate one to both parties. For weeks previous to the discovery the prisoners, it appeared, had been at work, and from not fewer than seven rooms, all of them on the ground-floor, they had sunk shafts twelve feet in depth, and caused them all to meet at one common centre, whence as many chambers went off. These were driven beyond the extremity of the outer wall; and one—that of which the sentry was thus unexpectedly made aware—the ingenious miners had carried forward with such skill, that in two days more it would have been in a condition to be opened. The rubbish, it appeared, which from these several covered ways they scooped out, was carried about by the prisoners in their pockets, till they found an opportunity of scattering it over the surface of the great square. Yet the desperate men had a great deal more to encounter than the mere obstacles which the excavation of the castle of Porchester presented· Their first proceeding, after emerging into upper air, must needs have been to surprise and overpower the troops that occupied the

barracks immediately contiguous; an operation of doubtful issue at the best, and not to
be accomplished without a terrible loss of life,
certainly on one side—probably on both.
Moreover, when this was done—and that it
might, and probably would have been
done, no thinking man will.doubt—there
remained for the fugitives the still more ar-
duous task of making their way through the
heart of the garrison town of Portsmouth, and
seizing a flotilla of boats, should such be high
and dry upon the beach. Yet worse even
than this remained, for both the harbour and
the roads were crowded with ships of war,
the gauntlet of whose batteries the deserters
must of necessity have run; and out of which
no reasonable man among them could hope
to escape with life, supposing him to hazard
life, rather than give up all hope or chance
of liberty. In all sincerity, then, I am inclined to believe that the detection of this plot
was to both parties a merciful arrangement of

Divine Providence, inasmuch as the struggle would have been desperate, the mortality very great, and in all probability the whole would have resulted in the recommittal of the survivors of those who began the fray, to a more rigid confinement than that from which they sought to escape.

About a month after the occurrence of this adventure I got a furlough to visit my friends, with whom I spent several weeks very agreeably. I then rejoined the regiment, which had received orders only the day before to prepare for foreign service, and no great while afterwards it began its march towards the point of embarkation. There occurred, during the progress of that journey, a circumstance which not only distressed me a good deal at the moment, but in some sort affected the whole of my subsequent career of life. In my troop there were two non-commissioned officers— a Serjeant Waldron and a Corporal Rents, as different in their tempers and habits one from

another as if they did not belong to the same
species. Corporal Rents was a very noble
fellow—sober, steady, kind, generous, and
open-hearted. Serjeant Waldron was a
cross-grained, ill-conditioned creature, who
delighted in nothing so much as to annoy the
" Johnny Raws;" the elegant name which it
was his pleasure to bestow upon all who
might have recently joined the regiment.
With Corporal Rents I had early formed an
intimate friendship, and it was the great object of both that we should be placed on
parade as comrades; but the matter, somehow or another, was not arranged when the
order to proceed upon foreign service was
promulgated. On the march, however, we
made a point of being as much as possible
together. There was, indeed, but one man
between Rents and myself in the order of
files, and him I easily persuaded to change
places with me; so that all the while we
were upon the road I enjoyed the advantage

of my friend's conversation, as he enjoyed the advantage of mine. Nevertheless, we were not long permitted to proceed thus unmolested; Serjeant Waldron took little pleasure in our discussions, inasmuch as they partook in no respect of the ribald and loose converse which in those days, at least, was too much in fashion among soldiers; and he marked his disapprobation of our tone, by ordering me back to my proper place in the line of march. Like a young soldier as I was, I ventured to remonstrate, saying that I merely wanted to chat a little with the corporal, and would get into my place whenever a halt should be ordered. At this he became very savage, and repeating his order, desired that I would not presume to call the wisdom of it in question. " Now, Serjeant," said I, very foolishly, " what difference can it make to you whether I or your own proper covering file ride next you?' " What!" said he in a rage, " do you still refuse to obey ?" And so saying he clapped spurs to his horse, and rode off in search of the officer. In a moment a lieutenant of our troop—a very austere man, whose name it is not worth while to mention,—returned with the serjeant, and not waiting to hear a word that I might say, desired me to take my proper station in the column, and to be put down for the baggage-guard when the march should end. I was excessively indignant at this; but what could I do? At first I determined not to take this extra guard, to merit which I had done nothing; but a little calm reflection convinced me of the folly of such a resolution, and I made up my mind that it would be best for me to submit with patience to whatever load my superiors might impose.

I took my proper place in the line of march, and at the close of the movement received notice that at ten o'clock it would be my turn to mount sentry under the market-place. Meanwhile I adjourned with my comrades to the quarters which had been assigned us, and drinking freely with them, never thought of stirring till the clock had struck ten. Then, however, I jumped up, paid my reckoning, and ran off to the market-place, which, being close at hand, I must have reached within a minute or two of the time appointed for my appearance there. A corporal was in command, greatly resembling in his habits and temper my friend Serjeant Waldron. "Are you aware," said he, "how late it is? You are a full half hour behind your time, and I have put another man in your place as sentry. I shall confine you, and make a report of the circumstance to the captain in the morning. You are drunk, sir, as well as late."

It was to no purpose that I assured the corporal of my absolute innocence of the offence with which he last charged me; and protested that the clock had just struck ten in the quarter whither I had been sent. He would not listen to me for a moment, but, putting me under arrest, stated the case, doubtless in terms as strong as he could find, to the captain. I was at this time a very young soldier—neither, from the hour of my enlistment, had I ever been confined before; so the disgrace sat heavily upon me, and I fretted over it. But no important evil arose, at least directly, out of it. The following morning I took my place in the ranks, which I was permitted to retain all the way to Honiton, and from which, it is right to add, I was never, after all, removed. While we lay in this place, however, waiting for the transports to be fitted up, which were destined to carry us to the seat of war, the captain sent for me, and severely reprimanded me for the crimes of which I was charged with being guilty. He said that he was not only vexed but surprised to hear such things of me, whom he had taught himself to consider as one of the most sober men in the troop; and he charged me, as I hoped for encouragement, and desired not to incur its opposite, never to be found in so disgraceful a situation again. Hard, hard was the task of gulping all this down, while my own conscience told me that the charges were quite groundless; yet I felt at the moment that to deny them would be profitless—so I put the padlock on my soul, and remained silent. I earnestly advise all young soldiers first of all to win the good opinion of their captain, and then, at every sacrifice of immediate gratification, to preserve it. The captain has every thing in his power, both to promote and to retard the soldier's advancement; and if you once get into his black books, it will cost you many a day of anxiety, and a considerable display of luck in your favour, to get out of them again.

I remember that about this time I received a very acceptable present from home, in the shape of various articles that would be useful during the voyage, as well as some money and tobacco, which I freely divided with my comrades, and for which they were very grateful. This was hardly done, when we proceeded to Plymouth, where the ships were fitted up and lying to receive us; but of their state of preparation we could very little avail ourselves, inasmuch as the wind was, and long continued to be, adverse. Under these circumstances, it was a sort of privilege to me, that, having for my comrade a young man intimately acquainted with the mysteries of boatmanship, I was joined to him, and had it in charge to execute the officers' commissions, as well as to purchase vegetables daily for the men in the same transport. I recollect, too, that the doctor having taken his passage on board of our ship, was, by my comrade and myself, pulled, day after day, round the different vessels among which our people were distributed; and that our excursions were not always unfruitful; at least in the accession of creature comforts. But this order of things was happily not destined to last for ever. The wind shifted in due time, and an enormous fleet, amounting, on a moderate computation, to not less than one hundred sail of all sizes and descriptions, hauled in their anchors at a given signal, and, under a very slender convoy, put to sea.

Generally speaking, there is not much in the voyage from England to the seat of war, which, in the life of a soldier, deserves to be recorded. In my own particular case, however, the rule can scarce be said to have held good; for, first, having on a certain occasion towed a dead horse ashore, I was one of a boat's crew that with difficulty regained the ship again; and next, my old enemy, Serjeant Waldron, put me to a very great strait. It happened one day that he saw me playing with my comrades on the forecastle, and that, being in a singularly

bad humour, he ordered me below to look
after the horses.   I told him that I had
done that duty the day previously; yet he
would take no refusal, and affecting once
more to regard me as a mutineer, he desired
that I would remain below till he should
give me leave to show myself upon deck.
As a matter of course I obeyed, though the
old hands pitied me much, and protested
that had the dispute occurred with one of
them, they would have carried it through very
differently.   Still I went to the stables, and
abode there three whole days, and emerged
again into upper air only when it became
manifest, both to myself and others, that my
health would suffer from longer confinement.
A very angry man was Serjeant Waldron,
when his eye encountered mine near the
mainmast.   He swore vehemently against
my outrageous behaviour, would have forced
me below again, had not the rest of the men
openly withstood him, and ended by hurry-

ing off to the officer in command, and mak‑
ing a highly-coloured report of the whole
proceeding. It is not to be wondered at if
the officer should have adopted the ser‑
jeant's view of the case, he being an old man
and I a young one; or that, being assured of
my turbulent and mutinous disposition, he
should have consented to punish me next day
by the infliction of a picketing. But, though
Serjeant Waldron got all things ready, my
comrades sustained me with the assurance
that they would not permit the slightest
wrong to be put upon me; and their good
will, fortunately attained its object, without
bringing any individual of the number into
jeopardy. It chanced that a smart gale
came on that night, so that in the morning,
when the parade was formed, the ship rolled
heavily, and the serjeant going to call the
officer, found him deadly sick. With the
utmost difficulty he was persuaded to rise,
but he never got to the place where the in‑

struments of punishment were arranged. A
heavy sea struck the vessel — the officer
reeled and fell, and both he and Serjeant
Waldron were in an instant covered with
an ointment less odoriferous by far than
that of which Arabia is the source. Poor
fellow! our commandant was very much
ashamed of himself, as well as extremely
wroth with the person who had drawn him
into the scrape. He accused Serjeant Waldron of having occasioned his disgrace,
desired in a pet that the prisoner should
be set at liberty, and diving once more into
his own cabin, permitted both the crime
with which I stood charged, and the punishment that had been threatened, to be
forgotten.

CHAPTER III.

Voyage to Lisbon—State of the City—March to the Front—Wounded Men—Camp at Elvas.

THERE occurred very little during our passage to Lisbon of which it is worth while to take notice, or concerning which it may with truth be said that it differed in any respect from the ordinary adventures that attend men during the progress of sea voyages in general. We had the customary alternations of fair weather and foul, bringing with them their usual accompaniments of comfort and its opposite, the whole being summed up by a seven days' calm, off the coast of Vigo; and, as that was not the age of steam navigation, the seven days in question rolled but heavily away. Neither can it be said that a cruise in the jolly-boat, after an enormous log of mahogany, which with some labour we overtook, but were unable to turn to an account, gave much agreeable variety to the scene. Let me then carry my reader forward to the Tagus ; our entrance into which struck me as it does every stranger, with astonishment. I say nothing of the prodigious width of the river at its mouth; nor of the myrtle-clothed hills that greet your eye as you ascend: for it is on Lisbon itself so soon as it rises, like a queen, out of the water, that your gaze is with irresistible interest turned. And never, surely, has the young man's hopes more cruelly differed from the realities of life, than this fair city differs, as soon as you plant your foot upon its quays, from what it appeared to be while yet looked at from a distance.

As seen in the far-off horizon, Lisbon

looks like a city of palaces. The dazzling whiteness of the houses, which catch and reflect the sun's rays,—the series of terraces along which they are built, rising, in the fashion of an amphitheatre, from the river's brink,—the many spires and towers which adorn its churches,—all these give an air of magnificence to the place which prepares you to encounter, at every turn, marks, not of squalor, but of wealth. How cruelly the result disappoints you! Walls stuccoed over, with the stucco crumbling to pieces,—narrow streets, choked up with filth of the most horrid kind,—miserable wretches crowding about, as if they lacked not only the inclination but the physical power to exert themselves,—all these, with a thousand symptoms besides of indolence and squalor, and a national character utterly degraded, left us, on landing, no room to inquire how far our expectations in reference to the Portuguese capital had outrun the reality. And yet

Lisbon was in perpetual bustle during that season. Day after day ships arrived, bringing men, or stores, or munitions of war from England. The quays were continually crowded with soldiers, sailors, and camp-followers, while the river itself seemed to support a very forest of masts. Indeed, I never shall forget the splendour of the panorama on that day when our little squadron stemmed its strong current; for we met full in the teeth an enormous fleet, under convoy of the Caledonia, 110, and did not make our way through the throng without both giving and receiving some serious damage.

Black Horse Square will doubtless be familiar to many who honour these reminiscences with a perusal. It was there that, according to custom, we brought up; and there, after time had been given to arrange our accoutrements and get our harness in order, the regiment was formed. I was not so fortunate, however, as to march with my corps; for a

serjeant's party having been directed to proceed on foot with the officers' baggage, it
became necessary to intrust their horses to
the care of some of their comrades, and my
old friend, Serjeant Waldron, doubtless to
show that I was not forgotten, committed to
me the care of his charger. Now Serjeant
Waldron was an extremely careless man.
He had tossed his saddle, bridle, &c., he did
not know where, on first embarking ; and it
took so much time to find them that long
before I was in a condition to move, the last
of the horse-party had departed. Moreover,
when I did find them, they, or rather the
saddle, was in a deplorable condition; for it
had got into the horse's crib, and he, of
course, had not spared it in any way. With
some difficulty, however, I fastened it upon
his back ; and mounting my own, began,
with the serjeant's charger in my hand, to
thread my way in the best manner I could
towards Belem. But such a journey ! The

horses being young and skittish from long
confinement, pranced and kicked so that I
could scarcely command them ; and more
than once the saddle on which I sat turned,
through my inability to sit straight.   I question, indeed, whether I should have reached
my destination at all, but for the kindness of
an English soldier who happened to come up
just as, for the sixth time, my saddle had
gone round and compelled me to dismount ;
and he volunteering to hold the serjeant's,
I was enabled so to adjust my own beast
that all his pranks proved insufficient,
from that time, to incommode me in my
seat.   Then, following the guidance of my
friendly comrade, I pushed on; and, finally,
to my extreme delight, found myself delivered from a hateful office, and once more
in comparative comfort, because restored to
my regimental duty.

   I am not going to swell these pages by
describing matters of which a thousand ac-

counts, more or less accurate, have appeared already. Lisbon was to me what it seems to have been to my countrymen in general,— a scene of very little enjoyment; for though the climate is delicious, and fruit and wine are abundant, the manners of the inhabitants were, and I doubt not still are, pre-eminently disgusting. Of the lower classes I am bound to state, that they are at once the most indolent and filthy portion of the human race with which I have ever formed an acquaintance. With the exception of a peculiar tribe, called Galegos, who are not, by-the-by, Portuguese, but Spaniards, there does not seem to be anywhere the smallest disposition to industry among them. The consequence is that these Galegos, though despised and shunned by their townsmen in general, are by far the best-dressed and healthiest-looking people in the city; and, as always occurs in such cases, they are likewise the most civil and the best informed. In like manner, the women appear to entertain very indefinite notions as to the duties which devolve upon mothers and sisters in families. They have no idea of keeping their habitations tidy, but move about among the filth, which both within doors and without surrounds them, as if the atmosphere produced by it were not only familiar but agreeable. But woe to the individual, whether male or female, who ventures to walk the streets by night. Unless he be sheltered by an umbrella, not even a progress along the crown of the causeway will save him; for the good folks of Edinburgh are lame in the art, compared with the Lisboners—who discharge their vessels without even a " gardeloo;" and seldom miss their mark, provided there be a living thing beneath to aim at.

Nobody can have visited Lisbon without being struck with the frequency and magnitude of the religious processions which are there conducted. Of these, therefore, I need not take notice. But there was another ceremony—in its purpose, without doubt, humane and excellent, though in its results of doubtful utility—of which I am bound to make mention. I was struck one day with the sight of a string of eight or ten cars, each drawn by four fat oxen, before and after which went a crowd of persons, some well-dressed, others very much the reverse, among whom went sundry monks, bearing baskets in their hands, which they held up to the doors and windows of the better sort of houses as they passed. Into these the charitable threw loaves of bread, and other victuals, the whole of which being laid up in the cars, are transported, by-and-by, to one of the churches. There the monks mix the whole into caldrons, and convert them, with other ingredients, into soup ; for which dense crowds of ragged and miserable looking wretches wait eagerly at the doors. I found, upon inquiry, that the process went

on—I do not exactly remember how ofte
—but at stated intervals; and that the multitudes who looked to this precarious source
for a large share of their subsistence were
very great.

Of the dresses of the women, both high
and low, why should I make mention?
Wrapped up in their loose cloaks or man-
tillos, the former walk only to church, with
faces so covered that a pair of bright black
eyes are alone to be seen, and feet and ankles
of excellent symmetry.   Each of these is followed at a respectful distance by an aged
attendant, or duenna.   Whereas the poorer
sort walk alone in a mantle, formed frequently of scarlet cloth, with black velvet
trimmings, long sleeves, and white handker-
chiefs about their heads.   Long black veils
are likewise much worn, chiefly by respectable tradesmen's wives and daughters—who,
not unattended by their duennas, pass to
and fro without scruple in the dirty streets—

and from the merry becks and nods which these girls cast upon you as you pass, you are apt, if a stranger, to form but an indifferent opinion of their virtue. But in this you are quite mistaken. The Portuguese women are naturally frank and good-natured; so that a bearing which among us would tell against a young woman on the score of immodesty, is among them the common method of marking their good will towards the party saluted.

I have spoken of Lisbon as being, at that time, a scene of perpetual bustle and great confusion. The arrival of fresh troops, and the departure of men unfit for service, were matters of hourly occurrence; while a sadder spectacle by far met us day by day, when on the beach we beheld multitudes of unhappy women, who, not having been permitted to follow their husbands to the front, were waiting till their respective turns came, that they might return home. Of these all interrogated eagerly each new-comer from the seat of war, as he arrived; though their inquiries seldom referred to others than the individuals on whom they respectively depended. Poor creatures, it made my heart bleed to listen to the shrieks of some, when told that their husbands were killed; and to the sad low moaning of others, to whom the vague reply was given, that the party appealed to was incapable of satisfying their wishes. And then to hear them deplore their wretched fate—that they had not been able to follow the one human being to whom they were attached—that they must go back to a country where nobody cared for or knew them. I declare that, though little given to the melting mood, I have often been obliged to hurry away, lest my feelings should quite overpower me in the very middle of the throng.

One anecdote more I crave permission to transcribe, ere I pass on to other and more stirring matters. It will not, I dare say, be forgotten by any who visited Lisbon in 1810, that the river was night and day crowded with country boats, the owners of which made a harvest by landing passengers from the ships as they came in, and would not make way for the ships' boats; which, on the contrary, they obstructed. It chanced, on a certain occasion, that an officer, charged with important despatches, endeavoured in a man-of-war's boat, to make good his landing at Belem Slips. The Portuguese watermen, as usual, blocked up the passage, and neither his threats nor his entreaties, nor the assurance that he was proceeding on urgent duty, could prevail upon them to give way. At last he stood up, and called upon one of these people, who had placed himself directly between the boat and the shore, to move aside. The man insolently refused, and, grasping a boat-hook, made signs that he would resist the further advance of the Englishman by force. The officer lost all patience at this, and, drawing a pistol, shot the man dead on the instant. There was no delay after this in opening for him a passage. To the right and left the panic-struck boatmen drew aside, and he landing, proceeded on foot, unmolested to the place of his destination. But though the watermen were too cowardly to resent the death of their companion when it occurred, they made a prodigious fuss about it immediately afterwards. The corpse was carried in procession, unwashed, and in the dress in which it fell, through all the streets of the city; and money was collected from every passer by, in order to defray the expenses of the funeral. I never heard that any consequences more serious than this arose out of an affair which, in almost any other town in Europe, must have produced a bitter feud between the strangers and the natives. At the same time it is but fair to add, that there is no reliance to be placed either on the forbearance or the generosity of a Portuguese. If you happen to offend him, and a convenient opportunity offer, he will thrust his knife into your body without scruple; and where the odds in number are much against you, the sooner you take to your heels the better.

After a sojourn of ten days in the capital of Portugal, we received orders to march to the front; and went forward on our way in the highest possible spirits, and full of anticipations of glory and enjoyment. We crossed the Tagus in open boats, to a place called Aldea Golegas, and proceeded thence to Estremadura. There a furious thunderstorm overtook us, with rain so incessant and heavy, that in an incredibly short space of time the whole town became inundated; the water running in the streets a depth of a foot at the least, and sweeping into the cellars, where most of the poorer people dwelt, with the fury of a river. Our condition was of course cheerless enough, yet we bore it without murmuring, and would have been truly thankful, so early as the following day, to take it back in exchange for that which then befel us; for at the village where we halted there arrived on cars, about 700 wounded men from Albuera, whose plight was as pitiable—I might have used a stronger expression, and said horrible—as it is easy for the human imagination to conceive. No doubt they had received, when first taken in hand by the surgeons, all the care which the nature of their condition would allow. But they had performed since that period a long journey, through a barren country, and under a broiling sun—and their wounds remaining undressed all this while, were now in such a state as to defy description.

There was no lack of willingness on our parts to assist them. We soon cleared out the best houses in the place; spread straw, and, where we could find it, linen, for them on the floors, and gave ourselves up to the business of cleansing their hurts, the smell proceeding from which was fearful. Over and over again we were forced to quit the miserable patients in a hurry, and run out into the open air, in order to save ourselves from fainting; while they, poor fellows, reproached us, with a degree of bitterness which none of us cared, even in thought, to resent for a moment. I need scarcely add that among that mutilated crowd there were here and there strange specimens of frail humanity. One pair of wretches I particularly remember, an Irishman and a Frenchman, who travelled in the same car, both of whom had lost their legs—not partially, but entirely—and who yet ceased not to abuse and revile one another from morning till night. It was melancholy to hear them railing, in their respective tongues, and threatening one another in a manner strikingly characteristic of the two nations. Paddy doubled his fist from time to time, and shook it at Jean Crapot, while Jean would put his hand towards his left side, as much as to say, " Would that there were a sword in mine hand, for then would I slay thee."

We did our duty faithfully by our mutilated countrymen; so faithfully, indeed, that weeks passed away ere I was able entirely to overcome the effect which the distressing occupation had produced upon me. I could neither eat nor sleep, for every thing seemed to be tainted with effluvia from those cankered wounds, and my dreams were all such as to make sleep a burden. Fortunately for us, however, we were not long condemned to the torture; for war must be fed for ever with new victims, and we turned our backs upon those already smitten, on the morning after we had met them. Our next stage was Elvas, where, in a beautiful olive-plantation, we formed our camp; and beyond which we were not destined, at least for a time, to proceed. Moreover, as if fate had determined to console us in some sort for the distressing rencounter of the preceding day, we met this morning, while on the march, about 500 French prisoners; who, under an escort of Portuguese, were proceeding to the depot at Lisbon, and ultimately to the hulks. Poor fellows, we pitied them too; for the Portuguese ceased not to insult and abuse them—flourishing their swords over the captives' heads, and heaping all manner of offensive epithets upon them. Beyond this, however, they did not venture to go, because by this time English discipline was in some measure established in the Portuguese army; and English discipline, as well as English feeling, sanctions no act of cruelty towards a discomfited foeman.

CHAPTER IV.

The Light Dragoon and his Horse—The Guerillas—A
Battle and its Results.

Of Elvas and its beauties, including the
fertile plain out of which it rises, the noble
aqueduct which brings its supplies of water
from the neighbouring mountains, and the
forts by which it is commanded, I have nothing to tell which has not been told at least
a hundred times already. Moreover, mere
description is, in my opinion, of very little
use in such cases; for things which appeal
to the outward senses, must by the senses
alone be examined—that is, if the party curious concerning them be indeed desirous o
having his curiosity gratified. Besides, were

it otherwise, I am no master of the art of description. Mine was a humble, albeit a somewhat varied career, to detail which alone I have been induced to take up the pen; and so leaving the description of Elvas to those more competent, in their own estimation, to deal with it, I pass at once to the details of a private dragoon's life, as that is spent in the immediate presence of an enemy.

I am induced to think that the change from home service to real campaigning is much more striking, as well as far more difficult to realize, in the case of the light horseman, than in that of the infantry soldier. The infantry soldier finds himself, it is true, deprived, when he takes the field, of his comfortable barrack-room; while his provisions, instead of being served out daily, and by measure, may fall short from time to time, or utterly disappear. Then, again, he mounts guard—not over a stout brick building, which nobody dreams of assailing

—but in the open fields, where all his wits must be about him, in order to prevent an active enemy from passing his line, cutting him and his picket off, and bringing ruin on the army. In every other respect, however, his life is pretty much what it ever was. He must keep his arms and accoutrements clean, himself tidy, attend parades, perform marches, and fight battles as often as to his own leader, or to the leader of the adverse host, a battle may be desirable. But, except in the matter of fighting, he must do all this at home likewise; and if his bed be often the wet ground, and his canopy the lowering sky, why there is no help for it; he must make the most of them. The light horseman on the contrary, has not only his own wants, but those of his charger, to attend to; and the difference to the horse in the sort of life, which on service he is required to lead, is infinitely greater than the difference to his rider—supposing both to have been reared in England. In Portugal, for example, we had Indian corn served out as forage, which our horses would not taste, and which we could not get them to taste till we tried the experiment of soaking: moreover, we had to seek their litter where we could find it, to cut for them green meat, and train them to sleep picketed and in the open air, under which not a few broke down; and to bestow upon them in general a much larger portion of our care, than we had ever been taught, in the process of home duty, to consider requisite. In like manner, it was new to us to go on picket, and to sit on horses as videttes, for two hours on a stretch. It was equally new to our horses to have their saddles and housings fastened on for twenty-four hours together, and to receive their food with the bits hanging at their chests, and every thing prepared for action at a moment's notice. I do not mean to say, that where men's feelings or imaginations are interested, all this is not very delightful; on the contrary, there springs up between the rider and his horse, a companionship, to which there is no parallel in any one of the many varied connexions which human life in its progress enables us to form; and such companionship is always pleasant, whether the cord binds us to a brute, or to our fellow-man. But some imagination is requisite in order to carry us into this train of feeling; and hence you invariably find, that in the light cavalry at least, your imaginative people make the best soldiers. Moreover, as the light cavalry are always employed, wherever the nature of the country will allow, at outposts, both men and horses are forced to acquire habits of vigilance, such as to be rightly understood, must have been both witnessed and experienced. The cavalry soldier sleeps, like his charger, with one eye and one ear always open. Both must be quick to perceive the first flash of a carbine, or the first blast of the trumpet ; and both must be in a condition to take their places in the ranks, within a minute or two after the alarm is given.

Then again, patrolling, which is an especial duty, puts the metal both of men and horses to the test. You must move forward as if you had a hundred eyes: you must be cool and collected, and prepared for every conceivable adventure. Neither hedges nor ditches must offer insuperable obstacles to your progress, whether you be required to take ground to the front or rear; and you must be quite as ready and as willing to gallop off when to convey intelligence is your business, as to fight with carbine or sword, where you are desired to delay an enemy's progress. In a word, both the light dragoon and his horse are called upon, as soon as they take their station in the front of an army, to acquire, as if by intuition, new ideas on every subject; for, except in

the formation of column or line, and the art
of breaking up into order of march, and
closing into squadrons again, the home drill
—at least in 1809 and 1810—had not taught
us much of our real duty.

The light horseman who lays himself out
to become a useful member of his profession,
is sure to succeed. He will first of all de-
vote himself to his horse; and then his
horse as if grateful for the kindness shown,
will do for him in return innumerable
services. Thus, during a night march, when
the dragoon, overcome by fatigue, drops
asleep, the faithful animal will slacken his
pace, or sway from side to side, in order to
prevent his master from falling. In like
manner, if they be passing in the dark
through broken and dangerous ground, the
horse will often refuse to obey either spur or
rein: his superior instinct directing him to
avoid the perils, into which the ignorance or
over-anxiety of his master was about to

hurry them. Moreover, the horse knows his master's voice: it eats out of his palm, lowers its head for the wellknown caress, and licks his hand like a dog in acknowledgment. And when it comes to this, let not the light dragoon be afraid to trust his charger in every thing. If they be the attacking party, his horse will carry him bravely on: if it be necessary to fly, there is no fence which he will refuse, or which, unless it actually exceed his physical powers to surmount, he will not by some means either overleap or scramble through.

I was always fond of a good horse; and no sooner became aware of the necessity for exertion that was imposed upon me, than I gave up my undivided care and attention to the noble animal which I rode. He was young, but full of spirit; and though like the rest he soon fell away in flesh, I had the happiness to see, from the condition of his coat, and the spirit and alacrity which on all occasions characterized him, that his health was excellent: there was plenty of muscle and bone in him, with a fair portion of blood; so that set us to what work they would, I always got well through it. It was not so with many of my comrades; not a few of whom seemed to regard their horses as incumbrances, always except at the moment when the value of the horse was most felt, and when, of course, theirs, in nine cases out of ten, failed them. Let me not, however, be understood as applying this reproof to a majority, nor indeed to any large number of the men of the 11th; on the contrary, it was only among the drunkards and other bad characters that this indifference to the animal, on whose efficiency their own depended, displayed itself; and such men, place them in what situation you might, would have been sure to disgrace themselves. Still, I think that there were few who took so much pains with their

horses as I did; and that I lost nothing by
the superior knowledge in grooming, which
this fondness for my own beast gave me, will
be abundantly shown, as the reader goes on
with my narrative.

We had occupied our encampment some
time, taking our turns in outpost duty, and
occasionally skirmishing with the enemy,
when there arrived at our lines one day a
body of persons, whose uncouth appearance
and strangely anomalous equipment excited
in us to the full as much of wonder as admi-
ration. They were guerillas, or armed peasants, whom the French not unaptly describe
as brigands; of whom some had once been
regular soldiers belonging to the broken
armies of Spain, while others were petty
farmers, or the sons of farmers, chiefly from
the mountains of Estremadura. Of the com-
position of these corps, enough has been said
in other quarters to convey to the minds of
my countrymen in general a tolerably ac-

curate acquaintance with the subject. Created partly by the war, partly by the smuggling habits of the people, the guerillas did
here and there excellent service; by attacking convoys, harassing columns in their
march, and cutting off detachments which
were either numerically weak, or separated
themselves too much from the corps on
which they depended. As was to be expected, I found, on becoming more familiar
with the Spaniards, that there was no end
to the tales of daring and of cruelty, of
which one or two of the guerilla chiefs had
been the hero. Moreover, it must not be
supposed, that when I speak of the guerilla
chiefs, I allude only to such men as Mina,
Don Julian de Sanchez, or such like. Every
town and village in Spain had its regular
chieftain, whose exploits the youths and
maidens loved to recount; and who, in the
eyes of his admiring neighbours, was of
infinitely more use in clearing the Peninsula

of its invaders, than Lord Wellington and all his generals put together. Neither was it an unusual thing to find a priest at the head of his own band, of whom, by-the-by, it is asserted, that if they were the most courageous—of which there seems to be little doubt—they were likewise the most merciless of all who waged war, not as soldiers but as robbers. I heard it said, that about Irun and other frontier towns, the inhabitants used to keep a regular account of the strength of the different French corps as they entered Spain, as well as of the convoys of sick and wounded, which were told off to quit it; and that on the information derived from this source, the guerillas were accustomed to act in almost all the most successful of the enterprizes, which gave a character of its own to the late Spanish war.

Our friends the guerillas did not long abide among us, whose method of waging war accorded very little either with their habits or their wishes. They sought for plunder, and liked it the better when they won it at the cost of a great many lives to the enemy. We faced the French squadrons fairly in the field, and never dreamed of molesting them, unless some important operation should be in progress. It came out, however, in due course of time, that the French were not yet disposed to act on so lofty a principle; and indeed, though we were the sufferers, I cannot find in my heart seriously to blame them. The circumstances of the case were these:—

While we lay in the vicinity of Elvas, the enemy began to show in and around Badajos a large force, of which a considerable portion were horsemen. It was our business to watch them; and as the 11th, with a detachment from the 3rd German Hussars constituted the entire amount of cavalry then on the spot, our vigilance as well as har-

dihood was more than once put sharply to
the trial. For the most part we came pretty
well out of these affairs; but in the end, the
troop of which I was a member suffered all
but annihilation. It happened that when we
were on picket, a trooper belonging to the
Germans deserted to the enemy; and carrying with him accurate information relative
both to our position and our strength, enabled them, without hazard, to arrange a
plan for cutting us off. They marched, after
nightfall, with the greater part of their cavalry,—threw a strong body into a wood on
our extreme right,—and, keeping it there
concealed, made their appearance at dawn
in our front, with a force greatly superior
indeed to ours in point of numbers, yet nowise so formidable as to justify us in our own
eyes were we to flee before them. Accordingly a smart skirmish began; which lasted
without intermission three hours, and the
excitement of which hindered us from pay-

ing any particular attention to what was going on all the while in our rear. At last, however, some of us chancing to look back, beheld a formidable line drawn out, in such order as to bar our way completely, were we to think of retreating upon the regiment; for the left of the line rested upon a river, and the right leaned upon the wood from which the whole had, during the progress of our affair, emerged. It is marvellous how slow men generally are to perceive that they have got into a scrape. We never for a moment supposed that these were Frenchmen; we took it for granted that they were Portuguese brought up, we did not care to inquire from what quarter, but placed where they were, manifestly for our support. On, therefore, we went with our amusement, till the enemy in our front suddenly called in their skirmishers, and with four squadrons advanced to charge. We were quite incapable of making head against such disparity of numbers; so we gave ground section after section, turning to check the advance, and still keeping up a warm skirmishing fire as opportunity offered. "Retire upon the Portuguese, men," exclaimed the captain; "when they perceive that we are overpowered they will advance; and then, ho! for another push at these rascals."

We did retire upon what we believed to be Portuguese; neither did we discover our mistake till something less than a hundred yards of ground divided us; and then what was to be done. The odds were out of all calculation; yet we were nowise disposed to be taken; so at the captain's orders we closed our files, and rode right at them. Never were men so entirely confounded. It was clear that they expected nothing of the sort; for they sat still, looking us in the face, and never made a movement to meet us. The consequence was, that coming upon them at speed, with all the weight and acti-

vity of our more powerful horses, we literally knocked them down like nine pins.
Over they went, the horse and rider rolling
on the ground; while we, cutting and slash-
ing as we rode, broke through. But, alas!
for us, there was a second line behind the
first, which behaved differently. We in our
turn were charged, and the battle became in
a few seconds a mere affair of swords, where
there was no room to move either to the
front or the rear. The result could not be
doubtful for five minutes. Outnumbered and
hemmed in, we were almost to a man cut
off. Eight were killed on the spot, twenty
were wounded, and sixty-three good soldiers
on the whole, lost to the service. The only
man, indeed, who escaped to tell the tale,
was one of our officers, who, being particularly well mounted, made a dash at the enemy's line; and laying about him, opened a
way for himself, though not till he had received a severe wound in the shoulder.

In the course of that *mêlée*, many feats of gallantry were performed; indeed, the enemy's loss in killed and wounded was far greater than ours, inasmuch as not fewer than fifty, belonging to the latter class, were brought to the hospital of which we became inmates. But there was one man in particular, who died so nobly, that I feel myself bound, as an act of justice to his memory, to speak of him. His name was Wilson. In temper and disposition, he was the quietest and most inoffensive creature in the troop; who never had a cross word with any one, nor ever, as far as I could perceive, was put even slightly out of his way. Nothing could induce Wilson to lose his temper—nothing put him into a hurry; whatever he did was done as if the doer were a piece of clock-work, and the matter to be arranged something which could not possibly miscarry. Wilson was, besides, remarkably sober: he never drank even his allowance to an end. But if he did not drink

he ate with a voracity which I have seldom
seen equalled. Bread was his favourite food;
and before his single pair of jaws whole loaves
would disappear, as often as he succeeded in
laying hand upon them. But Wilson's career, both of fighting and eating, was destined
this day to end; and he fell thus:

I saw him engaged hand to hand with a
French dragoon: I saw him—for I was by
this time disabled by a severe wound, and
stretched at length beside others of my suffering comrades—give and receive more than
one pass, with equal skill and courage. Just
then, a French officer stooping over the body
of one of his wounded countrymen, who
dropped at the instant on his horse's neck,
delivered a thrust at poor Harry Wilson's
body, and delivered it effectually. I firmly
believe that Wilson died on the instant: yet,
though he felt the sword in its progress, he,
with characteristic self-command, kept his eye
still on the enemy in his front; and, raising

himself in his stirrups, let fall upon the
Frenchman's helmet such a blow, that brass
and skull parted before it, and the man's
head was cloven asunder to the chin.   It was
the most tremendous blow I ever saw struck;
and both he who gave, and his opponent who
received it, dropped dead together.   The brass
helmet was afterwards examined by order of
the French officer, who, as well as myself,
was astonished at the exploit; and the cut
was found to be as clean as if the sword had
gone through a turnip, not so much as a dent
being left on either side of it.

The fighting was now over, and there began a scene, of which I cannot think without
blushing for the chivalry of our adversaries.
Not content with taking our horses and arms,
or even the purses and watches of such as
possessed them, they proceeded to strip us of
our jackets, boots, and even of our overalls;
apparently bent, as it seemed to me, on leaving us nothing whereby we might be distin-

guished as British soldiers. I do not know
how far the system might have been carried,
had not our captain, who spoke French flu-
ently, remonstrated with the officer in command; upon which an order was given to put
a stop to the plunder; and to most of us our
jackets, at least, were restored. But of watches,
money, and boots, no account was taken; and
we were marched off, some of us in a very
sorry plight, to the rear.

The wounds inflicted in this trifling affair, were all very ghastly. Being inflicted
entirely with the sword, and falling, at least
among the French, chiefly upon the head and
face, the appearance presented by these man-
gled wretches was hideous; neither were we,
though in almost every instance pierced
through, one whit more presentable. It is
worthy of remark, that the French cavalry,
in nine cases out of ten, make use of the point,
whereas we strike with the edge, which is, in
my humble opinion, far more effective. But,

however this may be, of one fact I am quite sure, that as far as appearances can be said to operate in rendering men timid, or the reverse, the wounded among the French were much more revolting than the wounded among ourselves. It is but candid to add, that the proportion of severely wounded was pretty equal on both sides; indeed, I suspect that there was a greater number of our people than of the enemy, whom it was found necessary to transport to the hospital, by slinging them over the backs of horses.

I was somewhat surprised at the moment, and I confess that the feeling has scarce left me yet, that the French should have been permitted to carry off a whole troop of dragoons, in the face of a corps, with infantry and cavalry at least strong enough to interrupt them in the operation. I dare say, however, that the reasons which dictated so much supineness to the lookers-on were adequate,— at least, I am bound to suppose so; but, be this as it may, we were, after the fashion which I have just described, carried off under the noses of our reserves; the whole of which had turned out, and now stood quietly to observe the issue. We did not go, however, without misfortune having wrought its accustomed changes in the moral positions of those who partook in it. When I was lying wounded, for example, near the spot where the captain stood, (a lucky accident for me, by the way, inasmuch as it saved me from undergoing the same process of plunder with the rest,) I saw not far from me, my old enemy, Serjeant Waldron, covered with his own blood, and so disfigured that, till he spoke, I could not recognise him. He knew me, however, and calling me by name, besought me to lift him up. I plead guilty to the crime of having allowed the remembrance of ancient wrongs to come across me even then; and, in the height of my indignation, I answered him with an oath, and told him that I would have nothing to say to him. But my better feeling gained the mastery immediately afterwards; and I was in the act of moving towards him, when a number of the enemy pushed in between us, and I was hindered from fulfilling my intention. He recovered from his wounds, and died the following year at Briançon in France. My friend the corporal, too, who reported me on the march, fell in this skirmish. He was endeavouring to force his way through the interval between two French squadrons, when one of the enemy's officers, perceiving his intention, thrust at him with his sword, which entering under one ear, and coming out at the other, killed him on the spot.

Finally, it may not be out of place to record, that the lieutenant, who, to say the least of it, showed me no great kindness, lost his arm. Thus, the only three men in the corps whom I found austere, suffered in this affair, from which, with the exception of a severe wound in my sword-arm, I escaped unhurt.

CHAPTER V.

A March, long but not agreeable.

OUR destination was Badajos, into which
we had so sooner entered than we were all
interrogated respecting our names, ages, and
length of service; and the answers which
we gave being entered in a sort of register-
book, we were forthwith dismissed to our
respective destinations. The wounded had
an option between the hospital and the prison; and, strange to say, many preferred the
latter, partly, I suspect, because they had no
great faith in either the skill or the tender-
ness of French attendants, partly because
they preferred the society and companionship
of their countrymen to that of foreigners. I

was among the number of those who foolishly
preferred the prison;—and great and lasting
reasons I had to repent of it; for in the
hospital we should have had at least regular dressing for our hurts; whereas in prison we could only apply to each other's
wounds portions of chewed tobacco. To
me the consequence was, that my wound
healed too fast upon the surface, and skinn-
ing over ere a cure had been effected at the
bottom, it soon suppurated, and broke out
again. I need not assure those to whom
such subjects are familiar, that a wound
which breaks out after having been once
ostensibly cured, is always a thousand times
more troublesome than at the beginning.
For a full month after mine took this turn,
I despaired of saving the arm; and I am in-
debted for it at this moment chiefly, I believe to a good constitution, into the vigour
of which no excesses of any kind had made
an inroad.

During our stay at Badajos, we suffered a good deal by reason, not only of the indifferent nature, but of the scanty allowance, of the provisions issued out to us. Each man received, per diem, four ounces of bad goat's flesh, with six ounces of black bread; but neither wine nor vegetables were served out; and as to salt, we never knew that such an article had existence. I believe, however, that in point of feeding we were not by many degrees worse treated than the French themselves, who could derive no supplies at all from the surrounding country, and into whose magazines time had already made grievous inroads. Indeed, it was melancholy to see the whole face of the surrounding country in flames; for the Spaniards, aware that they would not be able to reap the corn for themselves, set it on fire as soon as it approached to ripeness, in order that the enemy might not be benefited by it.

Our sojourn in Badajos was brief—only

four days; at the termination of which we
set out, on foot, for Merida. We suffered
as may be imagined, terribly during that
march; for, besides that several of us were
wounded, cavalry soldiers are but little accustomed to pedestrian excursions, and the
heat was quite overwhelming. Our lieutenant, indeed, (for there was no distinction
made in the treatment of officers, from that
awarded to privates,) became at last so weak
that he fainted. Still, there was neither
time given to rest, nor horse, nor mule, nor
vehicle of any kind furnished for his conveyance. The French guard brought him
to by shaking; and he was forced at the
bayonet's point to struggle on—the captain
supporting him as well as he could, till we
reached a halting-place.

It was a miserable, ruined village, without
inhabitants, or provisions, or accommodation
of any kind; and into one of the dilapidated
huts we were unceremoniously thrust. We

were all famishing; for no food had been
issued ere we quitted Badajos, and nothing
of the sort was to be had here; yet we had
endeavoured to provide against the extremity, too, by gathering vetches on the
road-side as we passed along.   Neither were
the means of dressing them wanting, inasmuch as I had exchanged my boots with a
French soldier for a cooking-kettle and a
pair of shoes; and the vetches being duly
boiled, we endeavoured to make a meal upon
them, but none of us could eat them: they
were so bitter, that our gorges rose, and we
threw them away in despair.

The next morning by break of day, the
drum called us from our lairs; and a morsel
of black bread having been handed to each,
we fell in, and the march began.   It was
neither so long nor so fatiguing as that of
yesterday; and it ended at a solitary shed
—a sort of long room, in which the farmer,
whose house stood a little way off, seemed
to have been accustomed to store his oil,

for there were a good many large jars in one corner, all of them empty. Into two of these a couple of our men crept during the night—so cleverly, that the fact of their having done so was unknown even between themselves ; and as we did not discover their absence till we had performed a good portion of a day's journey, they were fortunate enough to make good their escape.

The third day brought us to Merida, which we entered by crossing a long bridge, built, I believe, by the Romans, and still used in the common traffic of the town. We were halted in the market-place, where crowds, both of the inhabitants and of French soldiers immediately surrounded us. The former expressed great commiseration for our fate—the latter gloried in our capture and were not backward in saluting us with such epithets as marked a feeling for us both of hatred and contempt. But they did us no serious injury: and as we were per-

mitted to halt here a day, our jaded limbs
gathered a good deal of refreshment from
the indulgence. On, however, we went at
last, towards Madrid, changing our escort
every third or fourth day, and leaving behind us one or more of our comrades at
almost every hospital which we reached.
Among others, a Portuguese major had on
one occasion the charge of us—a deserter, as
I need scarcely add, from the ranks of his
own army; and if, in some respects, he appeared inclined to show us kindness, in
others he cost us a prodigious deal of unne-
cessary trouble. Moreover, his was the
only command which gave birth to any thing
like an adventure. It was this:

We were not far from Truxillo, when
groups of strange-looking men, that kept
hovering about our flanks and in our front,
caused an alarm. They were all mounted;
but either because they considered our convoy too strong to be attacked, or that they

wished to draw us deeper into a wild and uninhabited country, they held, for a time, so far aloof, that none of us could quite determine what their occupation might be. We, that is, we English prisoners, believed, because we hoped that they were guerillas; whereas the major, though manifestly ill at ease, scouted the idea. But he was not destined to remain very long under a mistaken impression. The numbers of the stragglers increased: they halted on the road before us, and, spreading off to the right and left, bore down in a sort of irregular line.

The major no sooner saw this, than he detached a portion of his mounted force to oppose them. The cavaliers soon met, and forthwith a fire of carbines and pistols left us no room to doubt that a body of maranders were around us, and that our fate depended entirely on the courage with which they might push the enterprise. A council of war was promptly held among the English; and we agreed that, as soon as the affair should grow warm and close, we would rush upon the dismounted guard, which observed us, seize their arms, and give assistance to the guerillas. I do not know how far our intentions might have been divined by the major, for he appeared all this time in a state of the most pitiable alarm; yet he gave his orders with perfect propriety; and when in our rear a fire was likewise opened, he detached people in that direction also to sustain the guard. Then began a scene of awful confusion. We were a large convoy: there might be perhaps sixty laden mules, besides cars of various descriptions filled with goods; while our escort consisted of at least three hundred men, of whom upwards of one hundred were cavalry. But corps of even three hundred Frenchmen entertained the greatest dread of the guerillas, and the muleteers and attendants went very far beyond them in the exhibition of their terror. In a moment, the latter began to cut away the baggage, and to prepare for a more rapid flight on the backs of the mules. The cars, too, were in various instances emptied, and the bullocks goaded into a trot; while the parties both in front and rear gathered strength every minute, and the noise of the strife waxed vehement. It was then that the major halted; and seeing us collect into groups, advanced towards us. He used no threats; probably he guessed that we Englishmen were not likely to be swayed by them; but he implored us for our own sakes, and for his, to lie down upon the ground and keep quiet. We did as he desired, by no means relinquishing our own purpose;—of which the execution, by the way, seemed every moment to become more easy; for the guards, like their commander, took fright, and crept in among us as it seemed for protection. But, alas! for the realization of our hopes, the guerillas, as usual, fought for booty, not for honour. They appeared, also, to be perfectly well acquainted with the nature of the convoy— even to the particular waggons which contained the treasure ; and these having been abandoned, whether purposely or not, I cannot say, they gathered round them in a crowd, and advanced no further.

I have no language in which to describe our mortification, when we saw the Spaniards turn the waggons on the road, and drive them to the rear. The French, on the contrary, seemed beside themselves with joy ; while our commandant did not fail to praise us for our good behaviour, and to assure us that we should by no means be the losers by it. This was a poor compensation to us for the loss of our liberty. Yet we had not advanced half a league, ere we had reason to congratulate ourselves on our prudence, inasmuch as there met us there a battalion, which the officer commanding in the next town had sent out to meet us. Thus escorted we entered Truxillo, every window being crowded with heads as we passed beneath; and, being marched to the prison, we were there left for a brief space, to speculate on the sort of treatment that might be afforded us.

We had not indulged these anticipations many minutes, when the Portuguese major paid us a visit, to renew his expressions of satisfaction at our behaviour during the attack of the guerillas, and to promise us the indulgence of a day's rest as our reward. He assured us, likewise, that care would be taken to supply us with an abundance of provisions: and he was as good as his word; for, in as short a space of time as was necessary to bake the bread, a store of new loaves was handed in, with an allowance of fresh meat. But the Portuguese major was not the only person who seemed to feel for our

wants, and to be desirous of relieving them.
As evening closed, a quantity of loaves were
thrown in at our window by the inhabitants;
till we soon had enough to last us, not for
the day alone, but for a whole week, supposing the means of transport to have been
accessible. .In like manner two live sheep
were given to us early on the following
morning, which we lost no time .in slaugh-
tering, with bread more and more abundant,
all the gift of the inhabitants; and a fire
being lighted, and the carcases duly cut up,
we counted on a day of, to us, extreme enjoyment; but in this we were disappointed.
The major, either jealous of the good will
shown to us by the Spaniards; or, which is
not improbable, fearing that an attempt
might be made to rescue us, suddenly re-
voked his promise of a day's halt, and ordered the prisoners to be paraded. It was
to no purpose that we protested against such
a palpable breach of an engagement. The

major had the power; and he chose to exercise it; so there remained for us only to pack up as much of our meat as we could carry, and to take our accustomed places in the convoy.

Seven long leagues under a burning sun we accomplished that day; of which the effects were made apparent in the utter decomposition of our meat. Not having any other means of conveying it except suspended in lumps from sticks, it soon began to spoil; and had become, when we halted, so offensive, that we were forced to cast it away. Our evening's meal was therefore made, as usual, upon bread and water. Neither was there anybody in the miserable hamlet where we slept who possessed the power, whatever his inclination might be, to render our fare more nutritious. On the morrow, however, after traversing the field on which the battle of Talavera had been fought, we entered Talavera itself; and again experienced, in a degree more gratifying than ever, the liberality and kindness of the Spaniards. Far be it from me to detract from the excellency of the motives which swayed these generous creatures. I do not for a moment doubt, that we English, had we come alone, would have been dealt by exactly as befel, yet it is proper to observe that we did not come alone. · From the different towns through which we passed, our commandant gathered together all the Spanish prisoners that were in confinement, of which the number, when we reached Salamanca that day, had swelled to 300 at the least. It is quite possible, therefore, that the inhabitants, commiserating their countrymen, extended to us, in like manner, a share of the feeling,—in which case we were much the gainers by the misfortune of our fellow-captives. But, however this may be, soup, bread, wine, and fresh hay to lie down upon, were all brought in ample quantities to the prison; and of the three former luxuries we partook abundantly, and with extreme gratefulness. The latter, however, we were not permitted to enjoy; for again the jealousy of our commandant stood in the way; and, just as we had stripped and laid ourselves out for a night of sound sleep, the horrid drum called us to the muster. It was a cruel outrage this upon our exhausted strength. We had performed a fair day's journey since morning, and were ill able to endure the fatigue of a night march; nevertheless, endure it we did, over six. leagues of deep sand; and then, just as the dawn was beginning to break, we halted. Not yet, however, was any permanent rest afforded to us. The last stages between Talavera and the capital were, it appeared, peculiarly dangerous to convoys like ours; and our commandant was directed, in consequence, to steal a march upon the Spaniards, of whose intention to deliver us some rumour had got abroad. Accordingly, at the expiration of two hours we were roused from our beds on the sand, and commanded to push on; nor did we stop, even for a moment, till the suburbs of Madrid were gained.

It was the common practice of the French to show off their prisoners to the Spaniards, with the greatest possible ostentation. For this purpose they used to march us by circuitous routes, in order to carry us through the larger towns, and always took care to enter these at an hour when the mass of the inhabitants should be abroad. This good custom, it was not to be supposed that they would omit in the capital; and hence, though we arrived within half a mile of it so early as three o'clock, we were kept lying by the wayside till six, the season—especially on a Sunday—when high and low, rich and poor, are to be found in the public promenades, or seated at the balconies. Meanwhile, our guards set to work, furbishing up their arms, washing their faces and hands, and otherwise getting rid, as far as circumstances would allow, of the stains and soils of travel; and, finally, when the proper moment came, we were ordered to take our places.

I never shall forget, as long as I live, the circumstances which attended our entry into Madrid. We—that is, the English—were in a truly pitiable state. Covered with dust and sweat, ragged, unshaven, and foot-sore, we made but a sorry appearance, even beside the escort; and they, be it observed, were not over-nice in their persons. Yet we were surrounded, so soon as we passed the gate, by crowds of well-dressed people, whose very commiseration—and I believe that most of them pitied us sincerely—became, by reason of the earnestness with which they pressed forward to give vent to it, an intolerable burden. For myself, I was certainly not in a condition to receive gracefully the salutations of the fair. I had taken off my overalls on the march, and now stood in a pair of flannel drawers,—very black, be it observed, and somewhat scanty,—without shoes or stockings on my lower limbs, and having the upper part of my person covered by a helmet and a military jacket. As to my face and beard, these were what weeks of toil had rendered them. And yet I was quite unconscious of the ridiculous figure which I must have presented, till an old woman, forcing her way through the throng, suddenly caught me in her arms, and, weeping aloud, covered me, to my extreme horror, with kisses. It was in vain that I struggled to shake her off. She held me with so tight a grasp, that I began to dream of dying by suffocation: nor could all my efforts succeed in forcing the hands asunder which she had twined round my neck. Poor creature! I never could make out why these marks of affection were shown to me,

—whether I resembled her son, or was to her nothing more than a stranger in distress,—but that she meant well, the termination of the adventure sufficiently indicated. Having indulged her feelings as long as was agreeable to herself, she suffered me to go, and, slipping a pisetta into my hand, disappeared amid the crowd.

The proceedings of this old woman caused me naturally to turn an eye upon my own person, and I confess that I never felt so ashamed in all my life; for, of the multitudes who flocked round to gaze, a large proportion were young women, before whom I had little ambition to appear in the character of Don Quixote. Well pleased, therefore, was I, when the officer, after a quarter of an hour's halt, gave the word to move on—and more satisfied still, when the building which had been set apart as our place of confinement appeared in view. It was not very inviting, to be sure, in its exterior, yet it promised at least to hide us from an inquisitive crowd; and I therefore entered beneath its portal with a lighter step than I had as yet planted since I first turned my back on the position of the British army.

CHAPTER VI.

Prisoners' Fare, and Spanish Flirtation.

OF all the places of confinement into which I ever was thrust, this at Madrid was the most horrible. It had been originally a barn or storehouse; it measured about twenty feet by ten; and there was no other opening in it except the folding-doors by which we were admitted, and which at night were secured upon us. We found in it several infantry soldiers, belonging chiefly to the 3d Buffs; and the state in which they were may be guessed at when I describe the sort of furniture with which the prison-house was garnished. Some trusses of hay there were to lie down upon, not only worn, from long usage, into powder, but literally alive with vermin. Then, again, as the upper part of the cell was used for purposes which I need not particularize, the stench was horrible, while the squalid appearance of our countrymen told a tale of very hard fare, and the general absence of soap and water. With respect, again, to our diet, it consisted of the prison allowance, namely a pound and half of bread per day,—not made from wheat, but almost entirely from beans, and soaked, if we chose it, in cold water.

I have heard a good deal of the harsh treatment which French prisoners were accustomed to receive in the hulks at Portsmouth, and in other depots through Great Britain; but I defy any set of men to suffer greater hardships than those which were inflicted upon us during the whole period of our sojourn in this prison of the Spanish capital.

Our comrades of the Buffs seemed to have been long enough in confinement to tame down, in some degree, their spirits to their fate. They lay down, night after night, on the living straw, and showed no disposition to refuse us a share of it; but we could not bring ourselves to follow their example. On the contrary, we swept a portion of the floor, next to the entrance, as clean as we could make it; and there, on the hard stones, found such rest as they were calculated to afford. At the same time let me do justice to our captors. They did not prevent us from walking backwards and forwards, during the day, on the space in front of our prison, round which sentries were planted; and, slight as the indulgence may appear to persons more happily circumstanced, by us it was very highly esteemed. I verily believe, indeed, that but for these promenades, not one-half of us would have lived to tell how the enemy used to treat us.

We had occupied our quarters but a few days, when an officer, evidently of high rank,—for his dress was richly embroidered, and a numerous staff attended him,—paid us a visit. I am inclined to suspect that he was a person more elevated than he wished us to believe: indeed, I mistake the matter much if I did not see him, on a future occasion, enact the part of Majesty itself. But, however this may be, he read—whether Joseph or not—a sort of proclamation from a paper, with the purport of which an interpreter who accompanied him made us acquainted. It was an invitation from the intrusive king to join his service. It set forth that he was in want of volunteers, and especially of men accustomed to the duties of the cavalry; and it gave assurance of liberal treatment, and promotion, so soon as they should earn it, to such as might close with the offer. There was but one feeling excited amongst us by this precious document, and we did not scruple to make it known. The reader was greeted with murmurs and groans of disapprobation. Indeed, I went so far as to hiss, a salutation in which I was immediately joined by my comrades. One would have thought that an officer, even if he felt disappointed by the result, would at least have had respect for the sentiment of honour which dictated ever so unmannerly a refusal: but it was not so with the personage before us. He flew into a violent passion; insisted on being told by whom the hissing was begun; and threatened in case we sought to screen the culprit, that he would inflict a severe punishment upon the whole. I confess that I was not without apprehension, lest some of my fellow-prisoners would betray me; and I own that I expected such an issue from the infantry,—but I did them injustice,—to a man they refused to speak. Yet I am sorry to say that, in another respect, they were not all so true to their own honour. Two men—one belonging to the buffs, the other wearing the uniform of the 49th regiment—stepped out as volunteers for King Joseph's service; and, being carried away by the still angry officer, visited us no more.

King Joseph, if indeed it were he, kept his promise to our hurt. We were shut up in the prison for three whole days—a terrible punishment, it must be confessed, even if our offence had deserved it. But at the expiration of that period his wrath appeared to subside, and we found the barn-door thrown open, as it used to be. We did not, of course, fail to take advantage of the privilege; yet, except to myself, this little promenade was not the source of any adventure: and mine seems, at this distance of time, so ridiculous that I scarcely know in what terms to describe it. But describe it I will.

To the right of the prison-door was a street, which communicated with one of the great squares of the city, though by what name called, or by what class of persons inhabited, I never had an opportunity to ascertain. The street in question was entered through an archway, over which was a suite of apartments, and close beside it a flight of stone steps, where, during the three weeks that I remained in Madrid, I was accustomed to spend no inconsiderable portion of my time. A corporal of the 13th Light Dragoons, being, like myself, a prisoner, contracted for me a great liking, and lent me a book, which I read with avidity, believing all the while that its details were authentic. The book was neither more nor less than Gil Blas; and it took the faster hold of my imagination, because I made acquaintance with it, for the first time, on the spot where many of the hero's adventures are laid. With Gil Blas in my hand, then, I was in the daily practice of repairing to the flight of stone steps, where I used to sit down, and in following the fortunes of an imaginary person, cease for some hours to speculate on what might be my own. My perseverance in this custom at length attracted the notice of the people who dwelt in the apartments above the archway, and more than once I could distinguish the drapery of a female, who seemed to watch me from the casement above. Gentle reader, have some mercy upon a youth, whose head was so full of the stories of Spanish devotion and Spanish intrigue, that he quite forgot to take into account the absolute unfitness of his own bearing to enact, at that moment, the part of a cavalier. I confess then, that rags, and filth, and squalor notwithstanding, I took it into my wise head that some fair creature, dwelling in that elevated chamber, had fallen desperately in love with me. How I hugged the blessed vision to my soul! How brilliant were the pictures which I drew of her youth, her beauty, her extreme gentleness, her lofty spirit, and, dearest and sweetest of all, her absolute devotion to me! Gil Blas! Gil Blas was a commonplace character compared with me. I was on the brink of adventures which would throw all his into the shade. Accordingly, day after day I repaired to my wonted station, with a heart so full of its own musings that if ever I was myself in love at all, which is very doubtful, I was in love then with a being which my own imagination had created.

Not a syllable did I breathe of my happy state to any of my comrades. Even the corporal of the 13th remained in ignorance of the results to which his book had largely contributed; indeed, my plan was to become master of my fair prize in the first instance, and then to establish a claim on the gratitude of my countrymen, by making them all in some sort, partakers in my good fortune. For away upon the wings of the wind my fancy carried me, till I became a Spanish grandee at the least, and the prison-house was emptied of its inhabitants. Well, then, day by day, I repaired to my station, and each time I saw, fluttering behind the opened casement, the same feminine robe which had originally set my heart in a flame.

At length a hand and arm, covered by a long black glove, were thrust out. They made a sign to me—to me! beyond all question; and when I returned it, by rising and bowing my head, the hand was instantly withdrawn. "She is coming," said I to myself; "be still, silly heart—prithee, beat not so. She is coming, and I shall require all my energies to carry me well through the interview." She was coming, sure enough; for scarcely had I resumed my seat when a door opened close behind me, and I heard a shrill cracked voice exclaim, "Signor Inglese." I turned round instantly—but conceive my horror. There stood at the doorway a little old woman, as ugly as it is possible for woman to be, who held in her hand a bundle of cigars, and offered them, with a few copper coins, for my acceptance. Down, down, in an instant, fell the fairy fabric which for livelong days I had been building.

It was no enamoured señorita that had so often watched me. I had excited no tender passion in any bosom, young or old; but was a mere object of charity to one of the most odious-looking hags that ever wore soiled cap over unkempt locks. I declare that I was so completely taken aback by the revelation, that I could not so much as obey the old woman's signal, far less thank her. However, grandmamma was a good old lady, and would not be refused. She kept becking and becking, till at last I moved towards her, when, thrusting the cigars and coppers simultaneously into my fist, she muttered something, to which I could make no reply, and most unceremoniously shut the door in my face.

It would be idle in me to attempt a delineation of the feelings which now swayed me. First, there was a sense of keen mortification, then of the ridiculous, equally keen; and, last of all, a consciousness that I had behaved extremely ill to my aged benefactress—who, albeit she did not bring what I expected, brought the best which she, doubtless, had to offer. I reproached myself severely because I had omitted to thank her; and passing from that to a review of my own situation, I determined not again to put myself in the way of being mistaken for one who sat to receive alms. But the most severe ordeal of all yet remained to go through. Somehow or another I could not keep my own counsel, and, telling the whole story to my troop-comrade, I got heartily laughed at for my pains. To do him justice, however, Jack was very merciful in his mirth; he contented himself with advising me to return the book, the study of which had proved too great a trial for my wits, and sharing the cigars with me, we smoked them out, often pausing to laugh again at the ludicrous issue of my most romantic day-dream.

At last the order arrived for the prisoners to be mustered, and marched with a convoy which was then about to return into France. Well pleased were we when this announcement reached us ; for though the term " French prison" seemed to insure for us an indefinite period of confinement, our sufferings in Madrid had been such as to reconcile us even to that prospect, provided it brought not in its train a renewal of the hardships that were passed. Our arrangements for the journey, moreover, were very soon made. We had no baggage to pack, and, as to other matters, with these we had little concern. Unfortunately for me, however, my friend, the old woman, having, I presume, got scent of what was in progress, made me a present of a pair of rope-shoes, which I, forsooth, imagined would, when stuffed with cotton, prove peculiarly agreeable to a pair of stockingless feet. Accordingly I slung my leather affairs over my shoulder, and tying on the old damsel's ropes, placed myself in the line of march, and went on. But I had not proceeded many miles ere I discovered that I had committed a grievous mistake. The cotton soon got into lumps—the rope wore my skin into blisters; and I was forced, after enduring indescribable agony, to throw the old woman's gift away, and return to my leathers. I have sometimes wondered since, whether the old jade, annoyed at the cold reception which I gave her, did not fall upon this ungenerous method of avenging herself.

Our march through Madrid was a very curious one. About 700 Spanish prisoners having been added to our force, the procession covered a prodigious extent of street; for multitudes of Frenchmen took advantage of the escort which guarded us, and, with their families and effects, wended their way home. In addition to these, we had a prodigious number of waggons, all laden with the plunder of churches, convents, and even of private dwellings; while the armed force which guarded the whole could not fall short of 500 men. But these were the least remarkable features in the conduct of the little drama. No attempt being made to clear the streets, enormous crowds choked them up,—whose business, almost undisguised, it was to aid their countrymen in escaping. Thus, from time to time, a wave of human beings would break in upon the escort, with the efflux of which some half-dozen Spanish prisoners were sure to be carried off; and as these were instantly denuded of whatever articles of military clothing they might happen to wear, and had ordinary peasants' dresses thrown over them, it was impossible for the guard, bluster as they might, to recognise and recapture them. Then, again, holes were here and there cut in certain brick walls, along which our route lay, and prisoner after prisoner, leaping through, disappeared, and was heard of no more. I firmly believe that ere we cleared the capital not less than a third part of the Spanish prisoners had escaped; and I have more than once been surprised at myself that I did not attempt, by a similar process, to recover my liberty.

Our progress through the town, and for some little way after we quitted it, was full of interest; for we might say with perfect truth that it brought us acquainted with the entire Spanish nation. There, in their carriages, drawn each by eight or ten mules, went the proud and indolent hidalgos, their imbecile-looking countenances exhibiting no expression at all, and themselves attracting

no marks of respect from their inferiors.
Here walked the Castilian gentleman,
wrapped up in his ample cloak, with all the
dignity of an ancient Roman. Close beside
him strode the muleteer from La Mancha,
carrying a goad in his hand, and wearing a
sort of kilt made of hide. He was followed
by a group of Andalusians, whose long
brown vests, checkered with blue and
red, and their hair tied up in long silken
fillets, gave to them an air and manner
peculiarly their own. With prodigious vo-
lubility they were conversing, while their
quick black eyes moved hither and thither,
as if their speech, rapid as it was, could not
keep pace with the flow of their ideas. Then
again we encountered women sitting in the
corners of the streets, and dressing food for
these strangers. Long lines of mules, bearing
burdens on their backs, and bells at their
manes, which tinkled as they went; with
asses by the score, which one man was lead-

ing, while he talked to them incessantly, and seemed to be fully understood. And, to sum up all, the ringing of the church bells, the strange dialects in which the crowd was speaking, the swarthy visages of most, the sonorous utterance of all, gave such complete occupation to the senses, that reason and imagination both became paralyzed. We had no time at the moment to compare one idea with another; nor was it till long after that the full extent of the information they communicated became, upon reflection, known to myself.

Before I quit Madrid, and in doing so turn a leaf in my personal history, I may, perhaps, be pardoned if I place on record here a little piece of intelligence respecting King Joseph's habits and tastes, which I picked up—I am sure I have forgotten how—on the spot. Probably the reader is aware that the Spanish patriots, the more to enlist the prejudices of their countrymen against him, represented

Joseph, both in their writings and their speeches, as personally a deformed man. He was crooked, they said, and blind of an eye. Now Joseph might not care much about a libel on his beauty, were his beauty alone affected by it; but knowing how much importance his loving subjects attached to the circumstance, he took every means in his power to disabuse them of the fallacy. With this view he used to go a great deal into public. He walked the streets attended only by the members of his family. He carried tapers in many processions; and seldom or ever saw a person, no matter how humble, looking at him, but he turned round and stared the individual full in the face. Yet all his care availed not. The Spaniards derided the notion of his carrying a taper out of reverence for a religion which they believed that he had abjured; and, as to his blindness, they persisted, in spite of all that could be urged to the contrary, in declaring that it was real. Were the Spaniards singular in this respect? I suspect not. There is no arguing against prejudice, be the subject proposed for discussion what it may; and the conviction of the people of Madrid that Joseph was a Cyclops, amounted to a prejudice. Then let not these worthy people be held at nought in a country where men's greatest boast it is to think for themselves; and where all have been taught by experieuce the truth of the distich—

Convince a man against his will,
You'll find him but a doubter still.

CHAPTER VII.

How Prisoners are sometimes treated on a March.

THE march of a body of prisoners from one place of restraint to another cannot be expected to furnish much matter for description. Our progress, indeed, was marked throughout by a succession of hardships and sufferings, even to look back upon which never fails of exciting in me sensations the reverse of comfortable; for I hold it to be one of those popular errors which men mistake for truths—merely because they are continually repeated—that the memory of sorrows past brings present joy. Yet I must not withhold from my reader a few slight sketches, such as may enable him to form some idea of a condition of life, into which it is my most earnest hope that he may never, from personal experience, become initiated.

I have quite forgotten the name of the place to which our first day's march out of Madrid conducted us; but I well remember that the journey, from its commencement to its termination, was to me prolific of distress. In the first place, the sun shone out with an intensity of heat, such as constitutions worn down with hard fare and long confinement could ill sustain; while the dust, rising in clouds from each footstep as it was planted, got into our throats and lungs, and well-nigh choked us. In the next place, my feet, lacerated by the rope-sandals which the old woman had given me, became one mass of blisters. It was to little purpose that I removed the immediate cause of this evil, after the evil itself had been fairly incurred; I did not enjoy one moment's respite from acute pain throughout the whole of that and the succeeding day. Nor was it from this cause alone that I suffered. Convoys, such as that of which I then found myself a member, were accustomed to halt for an hour or two at noon, in order that the escort might be refreshed and the prisoners rested; the former by eating their dinners, the latter by sleeping on the ground. Like my companions in affliction, I threw myself down so soon as the long-wished for permission was given, but I could not sleep; on the contrary, I lay writhing in agony; and when the order came to fall in again, I was quite incapable of obeying it.

It happened that just as I was making an abortive effort to stand upright, a French officer approached, who, noticing the cause of my weakness, and greatly commiserating it, desired me to get upon a waggon laden with wool which stood near. "It belongs to our convoy," said he, "and will carry you to the end of this day's journey, at all events. Get up, my poor fellow, and take your rest."

I thanked him, and with the help of my comrade, managed to scramble to the top of the bales—but, unfortunately, I went not alone. Two or three of the rest, seeing how comfortable I had made myself, ascended the waggon in like manner, and lay down, like me, at length. But the waggoner had not been consulted as to the propriety of these arrangements; and we were soon made to feel that he regarded the matter in a different point of view from ourselves. We were scarcely settled, when he approached the vehicle, with an expression of fierce anger in his countenance, and forthwith, without having spoken a word, he began to belabour us about the heads and faces with his whip. My comrades, more active than I, soon leaped down. For me, I suffered in silence, for the height of the bales from the ground was considerable; and the bare thought of jumping upon my bruised feet was agony. I therefore took the blows, which continued to fall in showers upon me, with all the patience which I could muster, till in the end they wore me out, and I fainted. I believe that in this plight I fell from the waggon; at all events, when I recovered my senses I found myself lying upon the road, and, on lifting my head, I had the satisfaction to perceive that the convoy was advanced a long way to the front. What was to be done? I was even less capable of exertion then than I had been ere the halt took place. My very comrade, too, had abandoned me, and the rear-guard were preparing to quit their ground. Now the rear-guard had already shown, on more than one occasion, that they were determined not to favour the escape of any prisoner who should, under the pretext of inability to proceed, drop behind the column; they had shot, without mercy, every straggler whom they found it impossible to drive before them. What should I do?—struggle on, or lie still, with the certainty of death as my reward? I declare that the weight of a straw would have turned the scale to either side that day; for if ever man felt existence to be a burden, I did. Yet there is an instinct of self-preservation within, which will not permit us deliberately to resign life, so long as the chances of saving it appear to be within our reach. I made a desperate effort to rise, and succeeded; but as to moving on, that I believe would have been impossible, had not Providence sent a means of transport to my relief.

While I tottered, rather than stood, upon my blistered feet, a Spanish coach happened to pass; fastened beneath the perch of which was a spare pole, projecting a foot or two from the rear. A rope, likewise, hung from the top of the vehicle, as if it had been suspended there for my especial use; this I seized with a desperate clutch, just as the hinder wheel rolled beyond my station. I was swung to the back of the carriage instantly; and scrambling upon the pole, I made the rope fast round my middle, and felt that I was secure. Never has human breast beaten more gratefully than mine did at that instant; for the coming up of the carriage seemed to me to have been directed by Heaven for the preservation of my life. Neither was I indifferent to the fate of others; for observing, not long afterwards that another of our men had fallen, and was, like myself, entirely exhausted, I shouted out to him so soon as the carriage approached the spot where he lay, and invited him to join me, which, with a desperate effort, he did. I made room for him on the pole. By then untying the rope, and passing it round our middles, both were made fast, and we jogged on, uneasily enough, as the judicious reader will believe, yet very thankful for the blessing, such as it was, which a kind Providence had thrown in our way.

We had journeyed thus about three English miles, when the same officer who had advised me to ascend the waggon rode up. He instantly recognised me, but not only did not require either of us to descend, but expressed himself well pleased that I had found a substitute for the resting-place from which the waggoner had driven me. Neither did his kindness end there. The carriage was his own; it contained his wife and two children, whom he was escorting back into France, and who carried with them their own provisions, which they were accustomed to cook over night, and to eat upon the march. He ordered the driver to stop, rode up to the coach-window, made his lady pour out two cups of wine, and brought them, with some slices of bread and sausages, to us. We ate and drank with grateful hearts, and received from the repast so much refreshment, that we found ourselves, when occasion required, fully capable of walking; and the occasion did present itself somewhat sooner than we could have wished, for the coachman, to make up for lost time, drove his horses into a trot, and the end of the pole—an uneasy seat at the best—was no longer endurable. We were forced to abandon our position. Nevertheless we held on by the rope, which dragged us into a run, during which blisters and bruises were alike disregarded; and we arrived in good time at the yard within which the rest of the prisoners had been thrust, not, to all appearance, greatly more distressed than the strongest of them.

I asked for no portion of my comrades' rations that night. I was too much exhausted even to eat; but throwing myself down upon the ground, with a stone for my pillow, I soon fell asleep. At daybreak

next morning we were roused as usual, and
the march began; the guards pushing us forward with very little regard either to our
comfort or their own reputation for humanity.
In my own case, however, it seemed as if the
endurance of the preceding day had hardened me for all that was to follow; for I
felt, to my great surprise, comparatively
well, and trudged on—not indeed at ease,
but suffering far less, even from blistered feet
than many of those around me. Moreover, I
observed that the Spaniards, however accustomed they might be to the burning suns of
their own country, were far less capable of
sustaining fatigue than the English. For
one of our people that dropped behind, a
score of these unfortunate wretches were
knocked up; and he in the Spanish garb who
once gave in never found an opportunity to
recover. I believe that this shocking practice of shooting their exhausted prisoners
was resorted to by the French in reprisal

of similar atrocities perpetrated upon their countrymen by the Spaniards. The French themselves, at least, so accounted for the barbarism; but, however this may be, I am sure that no good results arose out of it—inasmuch as the mutual antipathies of the two people became only, from day to day, more confirmed. I regret to be obliged to add, that this day an English prisoner suffered the same fate—and yet I had the best reason for believing that his executioner slew him in ignorance. The facts were these:

A soldier of my own regiment, whose clothes had melted from his back, contrived, somehow or another, to get possession of a Spanish dress, which he wore upon the march; and on account of which, as it happened to be in excellent repair, he became an object of something like envy to his more destitute companions. Poor fellow! his constitution was not by nature so robust as mine; and he repeatedly declared that, let come what might, it was impossible for him to proceed further. We encouraged him as well as we could; we took it by turns to lend him our arms: but all would not do. At the foot of an enormous mountain, which it was necessary to cross, in order to reach the place of our destination for the night, the pleasant town of Segovia, he sat down by the way-side, and resigned himself to his fate. There was not strength enough in us to carry him. There were neither horses, nor mules, nor cars for the conveyance of the feeble; we had, therefore, nothing for it but to commit him to God's keeping, and to march on. But God saw that this day he had run out the measure of time that was. allotted to him; and his labours, and his anxieties, and his hopes, and his fears, were all brought to an end.

It happened that my comrade and I, feeling unusually fresh, took it into our heads to diverge from the proper line of march; and making for an elbow of the mountain, began to climb, under the expectation that we should thus head the column, and find time to rest at the summit. We were not deceived in this expectation; and yet we were both tempted, by-and-by, to regret that we yielded to the impulse: for, though we reached the mountain's brow, and found a luxurious bank of soft herbage to recline upon, the spectacle which met our gaze, as we looked down upon the plain beneath, was harrowing in the extreme. The rear-guard of a convoy, of which prisoners of war form a part, marches, be it observed, a long way behind the closing files of the column. I believe that this wide interval is interposed between them and the captives for the humane purpose of giving to the feeble among the latter as good a chance for recovery as may be; but it does not always succeed. To-day, for example, we were horrified by observing—far, **far** away, in the distance—one little column of smoke rise after another, even when by us no report of musketry could be heard. But our feelings were not yet entirely harrowed up, for we had fixed our eyes in a great measure upon the spot where our poor comrade was sitting, and we were resolved to judge, from the fate which should attend him, of that which we apprehended might have been awarded to others.

I have no power of language in which to describe the breathless anxiety with which we watched the gradual approach of the armed party towards the base of the mountain. On and on it came,—another and another little blue column ascending,—and, by-and-by, faint and feeble, the sharp ringing in the ear, which told of a musket or a carbine discharged. Still we doubted the reality; for, as chance would have it, none of these things took place anywhere within half-a-mile of the spot where our comrade was sitting. But our doubts were not destined to operate for ever.

"See, Tom! they are approaching," exclaimed I, grasping my comrade's arm with a convulsive motion. "Look, look! there is one of them stepping out from the column; and now he approaches him. See, see! he stoops over him,—he is going to assist him. Oh! yes,—they will rise him up. But why does he step back?"

Let me draw a veil over what followed. We saw the musket levelled—we beheld the flash,—and, long ere the report reached us, our poor countryman rolled backwards to the earth.

The convoy reached Segovia, in a chapel at the outskirts of which we were halted; and right glad were we to find, when thrust into the interior, that the floor was covered with nice clean straw. We lay down, thanking Heaven for a luxury to which we had long been strangers; but the time alotted

for the enjoyment of it proved very brief.
One of us going to the door, overheard the
sentry talking, to his great surprise, to another French soldier in English. Our guard,
it appeared, had been changed; and we
were now under the charge of a detachment
from the Irish brigade, of which a scoundrel
named Smith was at the head. He was an
officer in the service of Napoleon,—a traitor
to his country and his legitimate sovereign;
and, like all such renegades, remarkable for
his hatred of the people whose cause he had
abandoned. From what passed between
the sentry and his Irish comrade in French
uniform, we learned that Captain Smith
was determined to take time by the fore-
lock, and, regardless of our sufferings, to
compass not less than seven leagues more
ere he permitted us to rest for the night.

Now we had already traversed six leagues,
of which a considerable portion lay over
mountains, and the seven with which we

were threatened scarcely dipped at all into the plain: our horror may therefore be imagined. Nevertheless, no good result attended our effort at remonstrance. To the deputation which we sent to implore his clemency he replied in language which I do not care to repeat, summing up all with this announcement: "I know that there is a long journey before you; but I advise you not to think of cutting it short; for I am a man of my word. No straggling, you scoundrels! remember, I have plenty of ball-cartridges."

It was useless to remonstrate with one whose nature seemed to be cast in so savage a mould; so we packed up our miserable wallets, took our places in the column, and at the word of command moved on. With one exception, this proved to be by far the most distressing day's march which we accomplished. The road—a mere track, which led from one hill-top to another—soon cut

our wounded feet to pieces. The rain began
to fall; and we, having but our tattered uni-
forms to oppose to it, were wet to the skin
in half-an-hour. Moreover, we could not
venture, let our necessities be what they
might, to diverge, even for an instant, from
the direct line; for Mr. Smith took more
than one opportunity of repeating his threats;
and we learned from the unfortunate wretches
whom he commanded that it would give
him positive pleasure to carry them into
effect.

I speak of these men as unfortunate
wretches, because I found, upon inquiry,
that they were not all naturalized Frenchmen, the remains of Emmett's and O'Con-
nor's bands,—out of which, as is well
known, the Irish Brigade had been formed.
One, on the contrary, I recognised as an old
acquaintance, who, after having lived as
hostler at the Greyhound in Blandford, had
enlisted in an English regiment, been taken

prisoner, and prevailed upon to take service with the enemy. This man assured me that there were several in the corps similarly circumstanced with himself, not one of whom had put on the French uniform except with a view to escape so soon as a convenient opportunity might occur. But such opportunities the French took care not to afford. " We dare not go beyond our cantonments," he added, " without running the risk of death upon the spot. For the gendarmes have orders to shoot us without trial; and we know, from experience, that they are ready to obey them. If there be any in your batch that are tempted to adopt this method of delivering themselves from immediate suffering, warn them from me that no good will come of it. I cannot now return to the condition of a prisoner; but, if I could, it would not be blistered feet, nor yet hardships tenfold more severe than those which you suffer, that would tempt me again to profess myself a traitor. Escape if you can, and die in prison if you cannot; but never take service in the French army."

I trudged on, pondering with painful interest the words which my old acquaintance had spoken; till, just as twilight began to deepen into night, I found, to my inexpressible relief, that the journey of seven leagues had been accomplished. Not even then, however, did the ferocity of Mr. Smith cease to display itself. Instead of affording us the shelter of some public building, (for we halted in a town of which I have forgotten the name,) he thrust us into a stable-yard, the soil of which was become, in consequence of the rain, a heap of mud; and, without straw or litter of any kind to lie down upon, without so much as serving out a morsel of bread or a draught of water, he told us to make the best of a lodging which was a great deal too good for such as we.

Upon the sufferings of that night I shall

never cease to look back except with uumi-
tigated horror. My bed was the soft earth,
—my canopy the stormy sky; yet I slept,—
though, when I woke, it was in a state so
benumbed and cold, that all power to move
hand or foot was for a while denied me.

I do not know how I should have recovered strength enough to stir from my lair,
had not a comrade, whose constitution seemed
more hardy than my own, befriended me.
This man, perceiving that I was quite chilled,
ran to a sort of sutlery, which was not far
distant, and purchasing a glass of brandy,
returned with it to me. I drank it as a man
may be supposed to drink water, who comes
suddenly, in the middle of an Arabian desert, upon a secret spring. I blessed the hand
likewise, that supplied the medicine, and
rose in five minutes greatly invigorated by
it. Yet I made but a bad march that day.
My feet gave way again: I was entirely
spent: and the first halt which we made,

on a wild and desolate moor, I threw myself down upon the ground, and wellnigh prayed that death would come to my release.

I was in this mood, suffering extreme agony from my feet, when, on lifting up my head, I beheld, not far from me, a spectacle which—be it spoken in all remorse and compunction of heart—served but to aggravate my distresses fourfold. Somehow or another I had detached myself a good way from my comrades, and, lying near a waggon, I saw a man descend from it, spread a table-cloth upon the grass, and convey to it a most inviting assortment both of eatables and drinkables. To these he forthwith addressed himself: and, oh ! gentle reader, if ever you have known what it was to gaze, yourself fasting, upon a feast that had been spread for others, then you will have some fellow-feeling for the agonies which, throughout the interminable space of perhaps two or three minutes, I endured. Both my appetite and my suffering were, moreover, enhanced by the sort of half conviction which took possion of me, that the happy man on whom mine eyes rested was not French, but English; for all his proceedings were redolent of the practices of that favoured land where the commonest peasant eats wheaten bread to his bacon, and never thinks of resting his jaws till his crop be thoroughly filled.

Heaven forgive me! but, over and over again, I invited myself to breakfast with the fortunate individual,—not once presuming to imagine that, be his nativity what it might, he would take the whim into his head of inviting me; yet he did. I daresay my gaze was abundantly expressive; but, however this may be, my surprise and delight defy the power of language to describe them, when all at once I heard him, after stopping the movement of his jaws for an instant, exclaim, " I say, comrade, are you peckish?

·If so, come and mess with me; there's lots
for both of us."

I need not say that I waited for no second
invitation. The influence of fatigue seemed
to pass away under the excitement of the
prospect thus opened out to me; and I
sprang from the earth with the agility of
one who had spent the night between a pair
of clean Holland sheets. I don't think many
such breakfasts have been eaten, either in
Spain, or elsewhere, from that day to this. I
declare that I felt quite ashamed of myself, so
tremendous was the onslaught which I made
upon the meatpasty and the flask of wine
wherewith I was invited to wash it down.

Having appeased the cravings of a well-
tried appetite, I entered into conversation
with my hospitable entertainer, who informed me that he was a soldier of the 10th
Hussars; that he had been taken prisoner,
'and released by a French general, who of-

fered him a situation in his family as groom.
This he did not feel authorized to refuse;
and he had lived for some time with his master in a state of comfort and respectability,
which made him wellnigh forget that he was
an exile from the land of his birth.

Having told me all this, he went on to
say, that he and his master were travelling
under the escort of our convoy, into France;
and that, if I liked it, he would reserve a
place for me on his waggon, and use his best
endeavours to treat me well throughout the
remainder of the journey. It is scarcely
necessary to add, that I closed thankfully
with his offer.

Hiding myself under the straw, I escaped
the observation of the guard, and was thus
pleasantly conveyed as far as Miranda, where
the cavalcade halted for the night, and where
I found an opportunity of being useful to my
fellow-prisoners, the bare remembrance of

which makes my heart swell, at this day, with triumph. The circumstances were these:

Under the protection of my friend Joseph, I not only travelled secure, but was, at the termination of the stage, treated with marked generosity by one or two French officers who seemed somehow or another to be attached to his master's family. One of them gave me a five-franc piece; another presented me with a foraging-cap; a third supplied the place of my dilapidated uniform with a good jacket and a pair of trousers; while Joseph himself, carrying me to the stables, showed me an excellent bed laid down, of which fresh straw and two or three horse-cloths constituted the materials. He then conducted me to one or two wine-houses, where we drank, in moderation, with the French soldiers, and found them not only agreeable, but exceedingly generous, companions. For example, rations were issued out to them that night—an allowance of bread and meat to each man; which they did not seem to value in the least degree, because, as they said, the Spaniards were bound at every stage to provide them with better. I asked Joseph whether it might not be possible to hinder the waste of throwing these viands away by begging them as a gift to the starving English prisoners. Joseph instantly stated the case to the French soldiers, and, without a single exception, they acceded to his wishes. The bread and meat were given to me. I carried them away to the bottom of a garden, lighted a fire, and, with the addition of some pot herbs, made a capital mess. With this Joseph and I made our way to the prison, and the joy and gratitude of its poor inmates filled my heart with strange feelings and my eyes with tears. I could not, however, venture to linger long among them, for I knew that, if discovered, I should be at once brought back to the condition of a prisoner. I therefore left Joseph to minister to their wants more in detail; and, after cordially embracing my comrades, retreated to the stable.

CHAPTER VIII.

The darkest Hour is nearest the Dawn.

FROM that time till the convoy reached Segovia I managed to share Joseph's waggon by day, and his excellent board and snug quarters at night. By some unlucky accident, however, I was detected, just as our vehicle was entering the latter place; and the couse-quences were, my immediate removal from the influence of my friend's kindness, and my return to the companionship, in every sense of the expression, of my fellow-prisoners. Not that Joseph forsook me: he visited me in our place of confinement at Segovia, bringing with him a flask of wine and a large loaf of

bread, and took of me an affectionate farewell—his master's route and ours diverging
at this point one from the other. We did
not part, however, till after we had exchanged assurances that, if Fortune should
ever bring us together again, we would without fail renew our intimacy. I am happy
in being able to record that Fortune did thus
favour us; and that she was doubly kind to
me, by enabling me, in a distant land, to pay
back, in some sort, the favours which I received from him in this my hour of humilia-
tion and suffering.

I do not know whence it came about, but
the further we removed from the Portuguese
frontier the less kind the Spaniards, as a
people, showed themselves towards us. At
Segovia, for example, the inhabitants, though
they provided their countrymen with good
things of every sort, brought little or nothing
to us; and we were reduced, in consequence,
to subsist as well as we could upon our scanty

allowance of very indifferent bread. It was but natural that the consideration of this fact should not be without its effect upon us. We began first to envy and then to dislike our companions in exile; and seeing them flush of money, while we ourselves were penniless, the idea gradually matured itself, " Why should not we, by fair means or by foul, share in their abundance?" When men are suffering real privations, and there are profusion and waste all around them, the moralist may say what he will, but they don't readily listen to the voice which would whisper of self-denial, and patience, and abstinence. We soon discovered, for instance, that the Spanish prisoners had large sums of money at their command, which they squandered continually in gambling, as if it had been applicable to no other use than that of keeping alive a violent excitement among them. I have often seen as many as forty or even sixty dollars on the ground at a time,

for which different groups were tossing, and
which changed hands over and over again,
according as the guess of this or that speeu-
lator proved to be correct.   At first we were
mere spectators of the pastime; but, by-and-
by, we began to argue that the money would
be at least as well applied in the purchase of
a few necessaries for us, as it seemed to be in
the encouragement of an idle and profitless
spirit of gambling among our allies. Accordingly, having watched till a tolerably rich
treasure cumbered the surface of the earth,
about a dozen of us suddenly broke the ring and
began to help ourselves, without compunction,
to the dollars and other coins that lay scattered around us.   The Spaniards, of course,
raised a clamour, but they attempted nothing
more; while the French, instead of interfer-
ing in their behalf, only laughed at them.
The result was, that, for several days, we had
tobacco to our pipes, and onions to eat with
our bread, while the gamblers, if not cured,

were rendered a few degrees more cautious in the exhibitions which they made both of their wealth and their cupidity.

In this manner we proceeded as far as Valladolid, where, numbers falling sick, and many more becoming lame through exertion, a halt of three days was permitted. It sufficed to fill the hospitals with invalids—few of whom, I have reason to believe, ever quitted them alive. But, however this may be, all who were in a fit state to travel marched, on the fourth day, to Burgos—whence a moderate stage carried us to Sallada, overwhelmed by the oppressive heat of the weather and stifled with dust. Here an event befel, of which, as it gave an entirely novel colouring to the whole of my after fate, I feel myself, in some measure, required to give a somewhat detailed account.

When thrust back into the common prison-house, I had been deprived, by the escort, of the few articles of wearing apparel which

Joseph had procured for me, and was now, in consequence, more squalid and torn than ever. I had no jacket at all—only a waist-coat out at the elbows; no shirt, no stockings, no cap: indeed, I was altogether as perfect a representation of abject poverty as the fancy of the most fanciful could well describe. In this condition I entered Sallada, and went with my comrades, to the prison yard, into which, by-and-by, came several French and English officers, the latter, prisoners like ourselves, though, of course, in better plight; and as it seemed, much thought of by their captors.

Among others, there drew near a gentleman in the uniform of a regiment of Lancers—a man evidently of rank and consequence, whom a considerable personal staff attended, and who appeared to have some object to gain by his visit. I saw him stop beside a man of the 13th; and, by means of an interpreter who bore him company, enter with that person into conversation. Not knowing why I did so, I listened to what passed between them, and found that the foreigner was desirous of engaging the Englishman to serve him as groom, and that the Englishman, though not personally averse to the arrangement, stated a fact which at once stood in the way of its completion. He told the interpreter that he was married and had a family; upon which that personage, though with great kindness, stated that, with a man so circumstanced, the count was not desirous of entering into an engagement. . He had scarcely said so, when his own and his employer's eyes falling upon me, both approached, and the interpreter opened with me the same subject.

I was completely taken by surprise. I assured him that I neither could nor would listen to any such proposition, but was determined to share my comrades' fate, be it what it might, till, by the course of a regular exchange, we should be enabled to return to our regiment. It is not worth while to fatigue

the reader's patience by describing how both
the count and the interpreter pressed the
point; for the officer of rank proved to be
the German Count Goltstein, who was at
that time at the head of the Lanciers de
Bourg, in the service of Napoleon. But
the results were, in a few words, these. I
believe that I should have stood out against
all his proposals, though they were both
numerous and liberal, had not an English
officer, who overheard the dialogue, inter-
fered to set aside my scruples. He assured
me that, if I was afraid of being compelled
to take up arms against my own country, I
laboured under a very groundless species of
alarm; that the Count Goltstein was a man
of honour—far more attached at heart to
the English than to the French; and who,
let happen what might, would not only not
urge, but never permit, my passing into the
ranks of the enemy. Finally, he and the
interpreter set such tempting offers before

me, that I did not know how to refuse them. I was to be at the head of the stables; to have charge especially of an English thorough-bred mare; to be well fed, well clothed, well looked after, and to receive as wages, or pocket-money, call it which you may, one guinea per month. Surely I am not to blame for having accepted this engagement, when the sole choice submitted to me was between its acceptance, and my continuance for some indefinite, yet, without doubt, protracted, space of time, a prisoner of war. But, be this as it may, I did accept it; and I am bound to add that I never found any just cause to repent of the decision.

A sorrowful scene was that which occurred between me and my fellow-captives, when I returned the same day to the place of confinement to bid them farewell. Some envied, others pitied, but all grieved to lose me; and my own heart bled as I squeezed their hands —not knowing whether I should ever be permitted to do so again. Yet I cherished the hope that, in my new situation, opportunities of serving them might occur, from which I secretly resolved that I should never turn away; and I thank God that I kept the resolution. Meanwhile, however, the count's interpreter, who bore me company, was beginning to exhibit symptoms of impatience.

"The count's quarters," said he, "are in a village two good leagues distant, and it is absolutely necessary that we should reach them before dark."

"But how shall we do that, sir?" replied I; "I have marched six leagues to-day already, and no consideration on earth would induce me to walk half a league farther."

"I do not wish you to walk," answered he; and then he went on to explain, that if a horse of any kind were to be had in the village, he would procure it for me, though the arrangement might not, it appeared, be without its difficulties, owing to the alarm of the

Spaniards in this quarter, who invariably abandoned their houses on the approach of a French force. The result, however, was, that he did procure me an animal,—a long-legged, sharp-boned mule, which he took away from a countryman when working it in a plough; and on the sharp back of which he mounted me. And thus, riding between him and his chief, (for the count himself, at the head of a troop of his lancers, waited for us in the outskirts of the village,) I made my way to my new quarters, not without having an endless variety of questions put to me respecting the strength and disposition of the English army; all of which I answered as vaguely and on as magnificent a scale as possible. But these are points on which it is scarcely worth while to touch. What can a private soldier know of the true condition of a force in which he is a mere unit? or if he did, how can the querist suppose that he will communicate his knowledge in its simplicity?

We reached the village where the Lanciers de Bourg were stationed, about nine o'clock in the evening; and I was immediately directed to the count's stables, where I was given to understand, that I should find a person who was capable of conversing with me in my own language. I proceeded to the place pointed out, and was a good deal struck both with the size and excellence of the stud, and the richness of the furniture, which was scattered somewhat carelessly about the stables. But the object which chiefly attracted my attention was a pot-bellied, rubicund, and evidently half-sober man, who no sooner turned his fish-like eyes upon me, than he hailed me with the exclamation, "How do you do, countryman? You be welcome!" I could perceive, from the peculiarity of his accent, that my new acquaintance was not English ; and I very soon heard from himself that he was German: that he had served in England as a private in Hompeshe's Dragoons, whence, on the dissolution of the corps, he had returned home, and passed into the count's service : for the count's estates lay round the village of which he was a native ; and, unless my memory deceive me, he was himself the son of one of the count's baurmen. Moreover, I heard him, with infinite pleasure, launch out in praise of our master's generosity and honour ; which came upon mine ear the more agreeably, that I did not listen to it fasting,—for my worthy comorado produced his cold tongue and his flagon of wine, both of which passed away famously; till, by-and-by, a sense of drowsiness quite overpowered me, and I besought him to point out a place where I might lie down. He was not backward in doing this. He called a servant, ordered him to make a bed for me in a room

adjoining his own; and conducting me thither, pointed out a comfortable palliasse, on
which I lost no time in throwing myself.
In less than five minutes I was fast asleep.

I do not know how long I may have lain
in a state of unconsciousness, when the touch
of a soft hand applied to one of my feet,
which was covered with blisters, awoke me.
There was a light in my room, which, on
partially opening my eyes, I ascertained to
proceed from a chamber-lamp, which a vene-
rable-looking hidalgo, with hair white as
snow, was holding in his hand, for the benefit of two young maidens in their labour of
Christian charity. These gentle creatures
were both employed in washing and dressing the feet and legs of me — an entire
stranger. One, indeed, they had already
rendered comfortable, by cleansing it thoroughly, and swathing it in soft linen, while
I was asleep: the other they were now in
the act of mollifying; and tender as their

touch was, even it broke in upon my rest, so lacerated was the member, and by long travel so impregnated with fragments of gravel and thorns. How shall I describe the delicacy and gentleness with which these high-born maidens extracted both from my flesh! And then they whispered words of commiseration and charity, which they would not utter aloud, because they feared to awaken me. I declare that I could scarcely credit my own senses, so entirely did the scene resemble the delusion of a dream. But the old gentleman, by-and-by, discovered that I was not asleep; and then the ladies, with natural modesty, stepped back, till he had reassured and urged them to their generous task again. The results were, that my bruised and torn limbs were thoroughly cleaned, and bandaged with the softest and finest linen; and that my benefactors pressed upon me a cup of chocolate, with some sweet cakes: after consuming which, I placed my head once more upon the pillow. And then—and not till then—the Spaniards withdrew.

I never saw these kind people again. I do not even know their names; nor can I guess at the motive which urged them thus to exercise, in my case, feelings of benevolence, which were manifestly congenial to their nature. But I suspect that they mistook me for a prisoner newly taken; and that their sympathies were the more powerfully awakened by the idea, that I was suffering all the bitterness attendant on a recent blight of my prospects. Be this, however, as it may, I heartily blessed them in my prayers that night,—and often bless them now, when the remembrance of their kindness comes over me. Doubtless they have had, and will continue to have, their reward.

I felt so comfortable after the dressing of my legs, and slept so soundly, that it was broad daylight when I awoke; which indeed might not have occurred even then, had not my German friend Kruger called me. He had evidently been drinking, and seemed somewhat impatient for the lack of my society; for he desired me to get up without any further delay, unless I were willing to go without my dinner. Now, the very sound of the word had been so long strange in my ear, that I experienced no desire at all to neglect the opportunity of improving it; I therefore rose at his bidding, and putting on the fragments of apparel of which I could yet boast the possession, I accompanied him to an apartment, in which the whole of the count's servants were assembled. At the end of the table sat his valet or steward; next to him the coachman; then the cook,— the very beau ideal of his nation, thin and spare, with sharp features, and a white linen cap upon his head; and by-and-by, as each could find a place, grooms, stable-boys, and menials of humbler degree. To me the seat

of honour was assigned, on the right hand of
the valet; for Kruger led me there as his
friend, and no one showed the slightest inclination to resist or resent the intrusion;
and the consequence was, that throughout
the progress of the meal, I felt that there
were few lots in life with which mine could
be exchanged, except at a disadvantage. For
my fellow-servants vied with one another in
heaping civilities upon me, and in loading
my plate with the most delicate morsels.
Then, again, the wine was both good and
abundant; we had our pipes and tobacco, with which to sum up all, and
we sat conversing by means of signs, for
not one word of each other's language
could we utter, till nearly ten o'clock at
night. At last, however, the party broke
up; after which Kruger, so completely dis-
guised that he could no longer articulate, yet
sober enough to point out a horse which was
intended for my riding during the march of

the morrow, rolled himself on his straw, and
left me to retire to my pleasant palliasse at
my leisure.

When I awoke next morning, I found,
somewhat to my chagrin, that the march
was already begun. The count, and all his
household, indeed, were gone; and on hur-
rying to the stable, I ascertained that the last
of the grooms, after sending off the baggage,
were about to follow. They had reserved,
indeed, for me, my own horse; neither did
Kruger appear to have forgotten me, inasmuch as a great coat and foraging cap were
laid, so as to attract my notice, in the hall.
But Kruger, like all the rest, seemed to have
given me the slip, whether because his own
duties engrossed him, I cannot tell. To say
the truth, however, the consideration of this
point occupied very little of my attention.
I harnessed my steed—a Spanish jennet, and
not a bad one; I took a long pull at the skin
of wine, which, by this time more than·half

exhausted, stood in a corner of Kruger's dormitory; and, vaulting into the saddle, began my journey, I knew not whither, in a frame of mind by many degrees more joyous than I had experienced since the day of my capture.

It was a bright, clear, sunny day, and I enjoyed my excursion extremely. Of my own corps,—if, indeed, the expression be allowable, when speaking of the regiment of Lancers which my master commanded,—I saw nothing throughout the day; but I overtook, soon after clearing the village, a column of French infantry, which served me in some sort as a guide, though from time to time rather provokingly. The French, when marching, will not allow any persons, except officers, to pass the heads of their columns; I was therefore stopped when making the attempt to get before the infantry, and had nothing for it, except to regulate my pace by theirs. Yet, I was very happy notwithstanding; and made an excellent meal, without dismounting, off the half of a cold fowl, which honest Kruger had stuffed into my great-coat pocket. Finally, at the end of about four or five hours, I reached the outskirts of a large town, on the bridge that led to which a serjeant of the Lancers was standing, who immediately recognising my horse, made signs to me to follow, while he should lead the way to the quarter in which the count had established himself. I need scarcely add, that I obeyed the signal with good will: to what purpose, the reader, if his patience be not exhausted, will learn in the next chapter.

CHAPTER IX.

I see more of the World, and fare better.

UNDER the guidance of the serjeant I soon made my way to the house in which the count had established himself, and found that he and all his servants were fast asleep. Upon this my steps were turned towards the stable; and the appearance of the stud, in point both of numbers and breed, excellent, yet exhibiting in their dirty coats manifest tokens of neglect, greatly surprised me. It was quite evident that not so much as a wisp of straw had been applied to any of their backs since they came in; while their feet were clogged by mud, and their hoofs filled, in the hollows, with gravel. This was not at all according to my notions of a well-ordered stable; so, making choice of the English mare, I led her out into the yard, and stripping to the skin—for, in truth, I was not worth a shirt—I set about dealing with her according to the most approved principles of grooming.

I was thus employed—having carefully washed her feet, and, by means of a brush, made her coat smooth and sleek—when the count, attended by his intrepreter, came out into the yard. He was prodigiously struck with the change of appearance which my careful grooming had created in his favourite; but I thought that he looked anxious, too, and I was not long kept in ignorance as to the cause.

" Is it your custom in England," demanded the interpreter, " to strip to the skin when you work? Our master is fearful lest you should catch cold, and begs that you will think of yourself."

I replied to this inquiry, as the real state of the case required, by explaining that I stood in nature's garb for the most obvious of all reasons,—namely, that I had not been master of a shirt since the day I was taken prisoner. Nothing could exceed the kindness and commiseration of the count when the statement was repeated to him. He sent the interpreter into the house for three of his own shirts, which he gave to me. He then presented me with a louis-d'or, and desired that, so soon as I should have completed my job, I would first refresh myself from the cook's larder, and then go and make such purchases as the state of my wardrobe might render necessary. It is scarcely worth while to add that orders so agreeable in themselves were to the minutest tittle attended to. I ate a hearty luncheon, refreshed myself by bathing in the Douro, put on one of my new shirts, and walked forth a prouder and a happier man than I had been for many a day. The next hour saw me in possession of a silk handkerchief for my neck, of four of a like texture for my pocket, of several pairs of stockings, and a hat; and, after all, I had silver enough left wherewith to treat Kruger to a good bottle of wine. In a word, my situation was as pleasant as it is possible for that of any man to be who feels that he is, after all, but a prisoner at large; and who receives at the hands of foreigners and strangers those marks of regard, which bring not with them their perfect value unless they come from our countrymen and our friends.

It is not worth while to describe how we continued our march, first to Valladolid, and afterwards to Salamanca. Pleasant excursions these were to me; for I rode my own horse, without having any other charge committed to me than to lead the English mare, which was my master's especial favourite; and not unfrequently my master himself rode by my side, and, through the interpreter, conversed with me. With respect to our living, that was of the best; and we invariably made choice of some beautiful glade or covert in which to eat our noonday meal. Moreover, in Salamanca I was measured for two entire suits of clothes; to convey which, as well as the rest of my wardrobe, a portmanteau was given to me. No man in my situation could, indeed, be more entirely comfortable; nor was I left without evidence that to others I was become the object of something like envy. But that is a misfortune from which I greatly fear that no successful candidate for advancement, in any situation of life, is free. Take the lead of your fellows, ever so slightly, and they may seem for a while to admire,—go on, heading them more and more, and they soon come to hate. So much for human nature.

We remained in Salamanca a considerable space of time; of which I did not fail to take advantage, by visiting every object in that

celebrated seat of learning which was described to me as worth the attention of a
stranger. Of the general effect of the city,
as it is first seen at a distance, with its endless
spires, towers, and domes, I need not say
much. The traveller, if he approach it while
the rays of the setting sun light up its gilded
cupolas, finds himself almost involuntarily
led into the delusion that the home of some
oriental prince is near at hand; and though
the idea may wear out before the lower gate,
is passed, it is succeeded by others scarcely
more familiar. For Salamanca, at least when
I resided in it, resembled no other city which
I have visited even in Spain. Its colleges
were then in their integrity,—its cathedral,
pure and graceful in its architecture, unin-
jured; and even the dwelling-houses, which
adjoined to the old Moorish walls, and over-
looked, by their narrow casements, the bat-
tlements which surrounded them, had a cha-

racter so peculiarly their own, that I find myself entirely incapable of describing it.

With respect again to the inhabitants, these struck me as having even more than the accustomed allowance of Spanish indolence about them. Salamanca cannot have been, at any period, a place of great trade. Like Oxford and Cambridge among ourselves, it is overhung by an atmosphere of academic abstraction; yet we naturally expect to find, where shops are abundant, some display of the spirit of barter, and neither in Oxford nor Cambridge are we disappointed. But in Salamanca the whole world seems asleep. You walk abroad in the middle of the day, and the streets are empty; you go forth in the cool of the evening to be met by hidalgos wrapped up in their cloaks, who, unwashed and unshaven, lounge from point to point, as if the act of moving were a labour all but insupportable. And then again for the women. They may have been better than the men; I verily believe that they were; but in the matter of dress, never have Eve's daughters so striven to disfigure themselves. Their long thin waists contrasted singularly with a degree of fulness both above and below, which quite surprised me; and their movements were, in consequence, such as might be expected, altogether ungraceful. I confess that I do not retain any pleasant remembrance of a city, which in its architectural arrangements presents a thousand beautiful features, and in which, as far as my own personal case was concerned, I had every motive for being satisfied with my residence.

In a place thus miserably circumstanced, it will not surprise the reader to be told, that I met with few adventures which made strong demands upon my interest. One, indeed, if such it deserve to be termed, I may be permitted to describe; even though the results were to affect me with no very pleasing ideas of the Spanish character, as connected with one of the most solemn acts in which rational creatures can take part.

I remember one day strolling into the cathedral, where I was greatly struck by the progress of a funeral ceremony, which had only just begun. The corpse was that of a young woman of some rank, which lay in its last robes upon a sort of platform in the middle of the chancel,—pale, and with the long black hair gathered in braids over the forehead. She was somewhat gorgeously arrayed; had a jewelled ring upon one of her fingers—possibly the gift of a betrothed,—and a golden crucifix suspended from her neck, while earrings, also of gold, were in her ears, and a brilliant clasped, or seemed to clasp, the band upon her brow. I did not get sufficiently near to judge of her beauty; but, as far as a cursory examination will enable me to speak, I should say that her features were regular; and that there was a soft, sweet, gentle expression in her sunken features.

The corpse, when I entered the church, seemed to have been just conveyed to its temporary resting-place—a platform, on which the black bier was laid. It had scarce settled down, if I may so express myself, when certain vergers approached, and enveloped it, all below the waist, in a black velvet pall, while a body of priests performed mass at the high altar, and a crowd of Carthusian friars sang a requiem for the dead with great effect. Innumerable wax candles burned both at the head and at the feet of the deceased. Her maid was in attendance beside them ; and the rapidity with which she crossed herself—lighting and extinguishing from time to time her own taper—seemed to indicate that she took a deep and solemn interest in the ceremony. Meanwhile, the grave, which had been prepared near one of the smaller altars, stood open ; and by-and-by a monk,

bearing a huge black crucifix in his hand,
approached it. This he planted at the head
of the orifice; and, as if his doing so had
been the signal that all was ready, a huge,
muscular, large-headed man, dressed in the
ordinary attire of a workman, and probably
the gravedigger, approached the bier. The
music suddenly ceased — the masses were
ended—and that barbarian seized the corpse,
which, without regard even to the semblance
of decency, he threw up, as if it had been a
bundle of rags, into his arms. He bore it
thus across the aisle, and, descending with it
into the grave, laid it in the coffin, which
yawned at the bottom of the hole. But his
business did not end there—the monster suddenly thrust up his arm, and drew towards
him, first, the lid of the coffin, and next the
black pall, with which he entirely shrowded
both himself and his future proceedings; it
is therefore impossible for me to say what he
might have done during the half hour that

he lingered in the grave; but I own that my imagination turned towards the jewels and the golden crucifix, none of which could I conceive it probable that he would leave to be devoured by the tomb. Nor was this the only transaction that disgusted me in the winding up of what, in its commencement, was an exceedingly striking ceremony. No sooner was the dead body removed out of sight, and the candles that stood beside the bier extinguished, than a spirit of extreme levity appeared to take possession of all whom the building contained. I heard the murmur of a light, and, as it seemed, a frivolous conversation pass through the crowd, while laughter, scarcely suppressed, told where each joke had taken effect, and spoke very little in favour either of them who uttered or of those who received it. Perhaps it might be prejudice on my part, but I own that I was thoroughly disgusted. I turned away, and walked home, not without. a conviction that, after all, there is more of real sublimity in the simple and affecting burial service of my own church than in all the mummery of masses and requiems with which the feelings of the heart seemed to be quite at discord.

Nothing could exceed the total disregard exhibited by the French for every thing which a Christian people are apt to consider sacred. Of the churches in Salamanca very many had been converted by them into barracks, and even into stables. In the former, you might see bands of soldiers cooking their provisions over fires, which they had lighted on the paved floors of the very altar-places, and fed with gilded wood, broken from the altars themselves. The smoke, of course, having no outlet except the doors and windows, rose and curled about the Gothic pillars, blackening the walls, and de-filing the carved work with which the roofs were ornamented; while the loud laugh, the

coarse wit, and coarser song, sounded peculiarly hideous in a place whence the voice of
prayer and praise might alone be expected to
proceed. But if the churches in which the
infantry had quarters were hideous, a thou-
sandfold more disgusting was the spectacle
presented by those into which corps of cavalry had been thrust. There, not the men
only, but the horses, defiled God's house, in
a manner, to look back upon which makes
me shudder. The floors lay a foot deep in
manure and litter: the marble pavements
were beaten into fragments by the hoofs of
the animals. No care was taken to preserve
the brass monuments, which, in one church
in particular, must have been, a short while
previously, both numerous and singularly
beautiful; while into the very stone walls.
rings seemed to have been driven, to which,
here and there, a brute more restive than,
the others was tied up.

They whose thoughts are continually turned towards the field of battle or the toilsome march, draw for themselves but an imperfect representation of the horrors that attend a state of warfare. It is when armies force their way into the haunts of civilized life,— when soldiers and citizens become incongruously huddled together,—when armed bands, that are accustomed to the touch of deadly weapons, stretch themselves forth to commit havoc,—and domicile and fane, and temple and town-hall, are alike polluted by the sounds and sights that appertain only to the camp,—then it is that war offers to the gaze of the looker-on its most hideous features; and our visions of glory, and renown, and high prowess, are all obscured by the contemplation of suffering and much wrong. I freely confess, that I used to pass these desecrated churches by in a frame of mind quite unbecoming the occasion. I said to myself, over and over again, " The miscreants who thus defile the temples of the Living God do not deserve to triumph, and triumph they assuredly will not."

There was a very large French force at this time in and around Salamanca,—according to their own account, at least seventy-five thousand men. It had been collected for some time, for the avowed purpose of driving the English into the sea; and now preparations were made for the immediate accomplishment of this much-desired object. Of these, while they were going on, I saw, of course, very little; though the extra work performed in all the bakehouses did not escape me. But by-and-by the truth came out, and the count himself disclosed it.

"We march to-morrow," said he, one morning to me, "on an expedition from which I, for one, augur no good. We are going to advance towards Lisbon; and, the better to ensure celerity for our movements, all our baggage is to be left behind. We shall carry nothing with us, either on the men's backs or

by the cars except twelve days' provisions;
and, before these are expended, your countrymen, it is assumed will be driven to their
ships. But, as I greatly doubt the issue, I
don't mean to take you along with me.
Remain where you are; take good care of
the horses; and, depend upon it that, ere
many days pass, we shall meet again."

I thanked my master for the consideration
which induced him to screen me from the
disgrace of even following in the train of
an armed force which was going to march
against my countrymen; and determined
that, as far as diligence and care on my part
could avert the evil, he should find no reason to complain that his horses had been
neglected.

The prediction which Count Golstein ventured to make ere the march began was veri-
fied to the letter. I saw the columns of infantry and cavalry defile from Salamanca,
with all the pomp and circumstance of war.

The horses were in good condition,—the men fresh, well-appointed, and in excellent spirits. The bands of the several regiments played favourite airs, and flags and banners floated to the breeze,—for the movement was begun with extraordinary magnificence. How different was the order of their return! In an inconceivably short space of time they came back, crest-fallen and dejected, having suffered quite as much from the lack of provisions and forage as from the sword ; for the system adopted during the first retreat to Torres Vedras was still rigidly acted up to. Every town and village was deserted on the approach of the French, —every morsel of bread carried away,—every animal removed, or else slaughtered; while the very corn in the fields was set on fire and consumed in order to prevent it from falling into the enemy's hands. The consequence was, that each league which they traversed in advance served but to involve them in deeper difficulties ; and, long ere the twelve days were expired, on which they had counted as securing a triumph, both leaders and followers saw that the case was desperate.

The historian has recorded in what manner the retreat to Salamanca was conducted. Horses died by scores—men foundered, and were taken or put to death by the peasantry, guns and carriages were abandoned at every pass. There was distress and anxiety everywhere. I shall never forget the soil-stained and demoralized appearance which the different regiments presented when once more they entered the town. The spirits, too, and tempers of all ranks were broken; and they seemed ripe for almost any species of outrage.

" I told you how it would be," exclaimed my master; " I was sure that evil would come of it. Your countrymen are as obstinate as the rocks on which they have planted themselves. They have handled us very roughy;

neither have I, in my own proper person, come off scot-free. That scoundrel, Kruger, has deserted with one of my best horses, and a portmanteau filled with some of the most valuable portions of my wardrobe. However, here we are; and we must make the most of it. How does the mare go on?"

CHAPTER X.

Forced Marches, and their Results.

THERE never lived a kinder or a more generous man than the Count Von Golstein. His own losses, his own privations, were invariably the subjects which engrossed the smallest share of his attention; and never was the disposition more completely shown, than now, on his return to Salamanca. The French had brought back with them very few prisoners; but among these there happened to be some men of my own regiment, of whose condition my master immediately informed me, desiring me at the same time to visit and relieve them as far as I was

able.   I went instantly to the tower in which
they were shut up; and the emotions to
which they all gave way, for they recognised
me in an instant, I cannot undertake to describe.   Poor fellows, they were footsore,
and half naked; and as men's hearts are
generally softened by the sort of misfortune
to which they were subject, they lifted up
their voices and wept, when they saw me
come among them.   But I did not come
merely to pry.   Having ascertained their
number, I hurried off, and my kind master
supplying the funds, I purchased a quantity
of meat and bread, which the cook and I
made ready between us.   With this, and
half-a-dozen bottles of brandy, I made my
way back—not indeed without considerable
risk of annoyance from the French soldiers
—who were quite as badly off as their captives, and whom the steam of the savoury
mess excited wellnigh to violence.   But as
I had taken the precaution to ensure the

convoy of the servant of one of the officers on guard, I succeeded in conveying my treasure in safety to the prisoners' tower; and the eagerness with which the food was devoured, and the keen relish with which they drank the liquor, sufficiently testified that to luxurious living they had long been strangers. Happy men were they in a few minutes: they sang, they chatted, they capered, and danced. In a word, and with the thoughtlessness which belongs to their calling, they forgot the evils that were past, and shutting their eyes to the certainty that evil would come again, they made themselves exceedingly comfortable in what the present hour could offer.

I rejoiced, as may be supposed, in the work of my own hands; neither did my power to serve them end there. My master desired me to select one out of the number, who might supply the place of Kruger, and be a companion to myself; and as my troopmessmate—by name Judd—happened to be there, I could not of course hesitate as to the individual whom I should select. Judd thankfully closed with an offer, of which I made him fully aware of the value; and accompanying me home, became forthwith both an active and a willing assistant in the work of the stable. Of the remainder, I never saw more till the peace of 1814: they were marched away early in the morning succeeding the day of what they called " the feast;" and Judd and I could give them no more than all the little money we had about us, and our best wishes for their welfare.

My mind was full of the situation of my poor comrades, when one day as I was riding through the streets, I found myself accosted in good set English, by a " How do you, countryman; what make you here?" I looked about, and saw a dapper little fellow in a civilian's dress; who, following up his first salutation, approached, and made immediate acquaintance with me. He told me that his name was Smith—that his father had married a Frenchwoman, and now followed the French army as a sort of travelling bootmaker, and that, by every body of every nation who made trial of his skill, he was admitted to be a first-rate workman. " But, come to the house where my father and mother live," continued he, " and I will introduce you to scenes that will amuse, if they do not greatly edify."

" I'm the man for your father and mother," replied I; " depend upon it I shall visit you shortly," and so we parted.

I confess that I had forgotten my new acquaintance altogether, when on the following evening he visited me at the stables; and as I had nothing better to do, I agreed to accompany him to the paternal mansion. It was a very mean apartment, in a very mean street, through the excessive gloom of which, I could with difficulty discover three human beings seated, two of them upon stools, the third in an arm chair; two were men, who appeared so entirely engrossed with cobbling, that they scarcely lifted up their eyes when we entered; while the third was a woman—as curious a specimen of the genus, as these eyes of mine have ever beheld. I could not hope, by any description, to convey to the minds of others an idea, even partially just, of the squalor of her appearance. I say nothing of her filth, though that was extreme, nor yet of her complexion, in comparison with which, saffron deserves to be accounted pure; neither will I speak of her apparel, which no Jew from Rag Fair, whom I, at least, have ever encountered, would have admitted within the portals of his storehouse. But there was a strange intermixture of cunning and simplicity in her eye, which would have tickled me much, but for the

tiger glance which from time to time super-
seded it.

" I've brought a countrymen to drink tea
with us, mother," said Joe.

" He's welcome," was the reply; " make
him sit down."

I sat down, and forthwith two broken
cups were produced, by means of which,
and a crazy teapot, we managed to discuss
some pint or so of slops. It was not Joe's
cue, however, to let the jollification end
there. He gave me a hint, which I did not
fail to take, by offering myself to stand treat
for some brandy—to procure which, Joe,
after a few modest denials on his mother's
part, was sent abroad. Doubtless the reader
has anticipated much of what is to follow.
The old lady drank cupfuls of raw spirit,
encouraging her husband and journeyman
to do the same, till the two latter fairly
rolled from their stools insensible, and she
gave evident tokens of a rapid approach to

the same state of helplessness. I looked
disgusted and somewhat alarmed, but Joe
only laughed at me. " Ply her well," said
he; " she is a perfect bag of sand, and a
good deal is needed to bring her to the
proper point; but once there, and for as
long as three or four weeks on a stretch, she
will continue in a state of absolute helplessness. Here, mother, take another cup; it
will do you good."

The old hag muttered something, drank,
and was conveyed by her hopeful child to
bed. She complained of thirst: he gave her
a fresh dose; and she fell asleep in a moment, muttering something about a stocking
all the while.

Joe clapped his hands, and laughed aloud,
while he exclaimed, " Now, my boy—now,
we have done it; and you, as well as I, shall
have your reward." So saying, he drew from
beneath the cushion of the arm-chair a stocking crammed with silver and copper coins,

dollars, half-dollars, quarter-dollars, and I don't know all what. " This is nothing," said he, pouring some of them out; " at the bottom of all are certain doubloons and louis-d'ors, for which I think that I can find a far better use than any to which she dreamed of applying them. Come, friend, help yourself: don't be bashful; nobody ever throve in the world that could not help himself."

I positively refused to touch a stiver; at which Joe laughed heartily; and, when I proceeded to remonstrate with him, his mirth only increased. · " Why, man," said he, " this sort of thing occurs regularly at stated periods. The old woman dearly loves both her money and the brandy-bottle: as long as she has resolution enough to keep the latter at a distance, the treasure accumulates, for she starves us all, and makes us work like galley-slaves; but, when the stocking becomes full, we always have a spree, which ends, as you see that this is going to do, by my making myself master of its contents. The old hag will not awake for these three weeks at least; that is to say, she will merely open her eyes and ask for drink—which I shall faithfully give her. And when she does get up, every thing will be forgotten, except that which I choose to tell her;—that she has spent all her savings in liquor. Why, then, should I scruple to enjoy myself, since nobody suffers?"

"But she is your mother," said I, in remonstrance; "how can you thus work upon her vices and abuse her infirmities?"

"She is as much my mother as she is yours," replied the hopeful; "and if she were, what then?"

My friend Joe's notions both of morals and manners were so very different from mine, that, with the termination of what he called "the spree," our intimacy ended. I frequently met him in my walks and rides, and learned from him that his mother kept to her time;

that she slept soundly for three weeks, and rose at their termination a greater screw than ever. But neither his arguments nor his entreaties could prevail upon me to share with him in the amusements which the plunder of the stocking procured. On the contrary, I felt something like compassion for the wretched old couple; and there, again, was in due time taught that I had been exceedingly weak for my pains. When consciousness returned to that amiable family, they found themselves, as a matter of course, destitute. To work they accordingly set, and, very much to their satisfaction, the old man received an order to wait upon an officer of rank, and measure him for half-a-dozen pairs of boots. But Smith the elder was destitute even of a coat wherewith to cover his upper man; and I, in an evil hour, was persuaded by his helpmate to lend him a new cloak which I had purchased. I never saw the mantle again, except at a distance; and then it enshrouded the form of Madam Smith herself, while she sat in her little donkey-cart, and accompanied the army on its march from Salamanca to Valladolid. I would have taken it from her on the spot; but she saw me coming, and with rare skill contrived to hand it over to her husband, who, being on foot, glided round some of the baggage-cars, and was at once lost to my vision. At Valladolid I made another attempt to recover my property; but it proved equally unsuccessful; indeed, I was overwhelmed on this occasion with such a torrent of abuse, that I had not the courage to face a similar infliction, even if the recovery of the cloak had been ensured. Besides, the brutes had utterly soiled and misused it; for it was their coat by day and their bed by night. I therefore gave the beldame a hearty benediction, and went my way.

We had not long occupied our new quarters in Valladolid, when intelligence of a rising in Astorga reached us, and a considerable corps, of which my master's regiment formed a part, received orders to proceed, by forced marches, for the purpose of repressing it. If the forced marches of the French army be conducted at all times in the order which distinguished this, it must be confessed that they make but light of the sufferings both of man and beast. We were formed every morning, and actually *en route* by three o'clock. At eight we halted and breakfasted; at nine we again moved on, and halted again at two to dine, and a couple of hours were then afforded to refresh; but at the termination of these the column moved: and it was always eight—often as late as nine or ten— ere we halted for the night. The halt, however, was not, at least at all times, a season of rest. There were cattle to be procured, killed, and cooked, for the morrow. There was forage to be collected, and the horses to be fed. There was not unfrequently the process of baking to be carried through; for we depended everywhere upon the supplies which the country could afford for our maintenance. Many a time have we found ourselves so occupied, by the necessity of attending to these wants, that midnight came ere we could throw ourselves on the ground, and catch an hour's broken sleep beside our horses. Yet in some respects the march was not disagreeable; and it was replete with interest throughout. For example, we, of the cavalry, leaving the high-road to the infantry and the guns, struck into all manner of by-paths, which carried us through a succession of vineyards, of which the fruit hung in large clusters, ripe, and ready for gathering. Again, it not unfrequently happened that our rear and flank patrols had the satisfaction of maintaining a continued skirmish with bands of guerillas, who fired upon them from the broken ground, and hovered round them like vultures watching their prey.

Then, again, the towns and villages, but especially the latter, were all but deserted as we approached; and all sent forth, as soon as our backs were turned, fresh bodies of armed peasants to annoy us. At the same time we were invariably met at the entrance of the towns by the civic authorities, who professed either to adhere to King Joseph, or, at all events, to be neutrals in the contest; and who hoped, by these means, very generally in vain, to preserve their own and their townsmen's property from violation. For, in good sooth, the French were fearful plunderers. It struck me, too, that the officers never made so much as an effort to restrain them; and the results were, that places which we found comparatively prosperous on our arrival, we left with all the evidences of rapine and violence about them. And desperate was the revenge which the outraged Spaniard took, as often as an unfortunate French soldier fell into his hands.

Neither wounds nor weakness roused his pity. He slew the straggler as if he had been a wild beast, and often added torture ere he ended him.

Sixteen days of constant marching brought us at length to Astorga; in and around which the corps proceeded to establish itself. The cavalry had quarters within the walls; the infantry and guns encamped outside; and strange and wild were the scenes which they alike enacted,—from which, as may be supposed, the ill-fated Spaniards were the sufferers. I must, however, in common justice observe, that the Spanish authorities brought the evil, in some measure, on themselves. They assured our general, for instance, that the town was destitute of stores, and that, unless he had the means of victualling his own troops, they ran great risk of starving. This was but sorry news for men who had not tasted a wholesome or regular meal for a fortnight, and were all but desperate in consequence. But a little exercise of the ingenuity habitual to our troopers soon refuted the declarations of the alcalde. Two doors from a large house which was assigned to the lancers as a barrack, there was discovered, in the *lumbre*, or ground-floor kitchen, a trap-door, by raising which a man introduced himself into a capacious cellar, well filled with all manner of stores, sufficient for the relief of one entire battalion. Tanned hides were there for making shoes, flitches of bacon, large bags of caravanceros, and skins of wine in abundance. As might have been expected, the success of this individual prompted many more to prosecute their researches; and our general had soon the satisfaction to know that he ran very little hazard of starving. Now, if he had been content to appropriate these stores, while at the same time he maintained strict discipline among his people, nobody could have blamed

him. The troops must be fed—so must
their horses; but he went much beyond
this. The soldiers received a sort of un-
spoken licence to plunder; and terrible was
the havoc which in their wantonness they
occasioned. Moreover, the honour of the
women, and here and there the lives of the
men, fell a sacrifice not unfrequently. But
let me not go on:—in the camp of the infantry you might see all manner of rich
hangings converted into tents. The soldiers
lay, or danced and sung among the tents,
arrayed in priests' robes and ladies' dresses;
while the lancers, in spite of Count Golstein's best exertions to prevent it, were not
altogether free from similar atrocities. Of
course the town became rapidly thinned of
its inhabitants, of whom all who were capable of bearing arms went to swell the
amount of the Spanish forces. Yet were
the French not yet cured of their propensity

to evil. They persisted in carrying on the war more like savages than civilized men; and they suffered in consequence all the outrages of which their own historians too much complain.

CHAPTER XI.

Burgos while occupied by the French.

WE remained in the neighbourhood of Astorga but a few days, at the expiration of which the order to march was issued; and, without having seen an open enemy, or had any opportunity of taking vengeance on a guerilla party, we began to retrace our steps towards Toro. There was no deviation either in the route, or in the rapidity with which we traversed it; and the consequence was, that our sufferings during the retreat were to the full as intolerable as they had been on the advance; and that, when we reached Toro, both men and horses—but especially the latter—were all but unfit for service. Among others, my kind, good master fell sick, and the skill of his physicians failing to set him on his legs again, he was ordered to try the baths at Valladolid. Thither I accompanied him, and on the interval which we spent there, I continue still to look back as on one of the most agreeable in my life of captivity. Valladolid is a large and stirring place: its inhabitants are much given to public amusements, in which I found frequent opportunities of joining; and lying, as it did, out of the broad channel of the war, both they and I were enabled to indulge our respective tastes freely and without apprehension.

My master, having derived considerable benefit from the waters, at length took his departure; and for a while we fixed our quarters, with the lancers, of which he was at the head, in the city of Burgos. Of the local situation of that fine old town I need not pause to speak,—with its hills over-looking it on each side, and its citadel crowning a rocky eminence, as if in defiance of the enemy who dared attempt to reduce it. But the condition both of the garrison and the inhabitants at this moment was so curious, that I cannot think of omitting to notice it,—more especially as the truth has never, to my knowledge at least, been told, by any writer, whether French or English, who has touched upon the subject.

It is well known that the hatred borne by the Spaniards towards the French had become, in 1812, bitter in the extreme. Taught by experience that they were no match for the invaders in the field, they waged war upon them by private assassina-tion,—insomuch that the French armies, victorious everywhere, except where the might of England encountered them, were nowhere, throughout the Peninsula, masters of a foot of ground beyond the limits of

their different encampments. In like man·
ner, the garrisons which occupied the towns
of Spain, were always in a state of siege.
There might be no organized force within
many leagues of them, nor the smallest
reason to apprehend the arrival of any
such. But each cottage in the suburbs,
if not in the heart of the town itself,
contained a little band of foemen, in their
own way more to be dreaded by far
than if they were openly in the field,
and banded together in companies and
battalions. In and around Burgos I soon
discovered that this was peculiarly the case.
At first, indeed, the manners of the people
deceived me quite; for I fancied that they
were content, because of the gentleness and
deference with which they appeared to treat
not me alone, but every Frenchman with
whom they came openly into contact. But
the experience of a few days taught me, that
this air of meekness was put on, for the sole

purpose of enticing victims into their power. There was scarcely a day passed without bringing in reports of assassinations attempted, if not perpetrated, upon our people. No man could walk half a mile beyond the town without being fired at; and even in the grand promenade, which extends along the bank of the river, and is shaded on either side by rows of noble trees, the same scenes were constantly enacted. I have ridden over and over with my master, to enjoy the refreshing breezes in that shady spot, and been driven out again by showers of bullets, which knocked the leaves about us, and came, we knew not from whence. In a word, the French were, both in camp and in quarters, prisoners at large, with the comfortable assurance continually forced upon them, that even within their own lines they could not count on escaping the knife of the assassin.

When we first reached Burgos, the garrison was labouring under a terrible and contagious fever.   The hospitals were all crowded; and every morning at daylight a couple of carts traversed the streets, collecting the dead from the wards in which they were lying, and transporting them to the place of sepulture. It was a ditch dug somewhere among the hills, into which the bodies were cast in heaps, no care being taken to treat them with respect, nor any mourning being made for their removal.   Moreover, several detachments were by-and-by sent out to levy contributions on the surrounding districts, and Burgos became, in consequence, the grand depot of French plunder in this quarter of Spain.   The Spaniards were neither unaware of this circumstance, nor ignorant of the process by which our treasures were gathered in; and in the beginning of 1812, they made a demonstration as if they had designed to appropriate them. The circumstances of the case were these:

One morning in the month of January—

I have forgotten the precise date, an alarm
spread that heavy columns of troops were
advancing towards the town. We ran to
the most elevated stations which we could
find, and saw, sure enough, 6000 Spaniards
at the least, marching in good order along the
Madrid road, and apparently bent on carrying the town by a *coup de main*. Now,
it so happened, that the town was at this
moment in a peculiarly defenceless state.
The castle, indeed, stood above the reach of
insult, not from this body of troops alone,
but from their betters; but the town was
no further fortified than by 'palisades, that
blocked up the principal entrances, and
light cannon so planted as to command the
bridges. Then again, the garrison, enfeebled
by sickness, was more than usually weak, in
consequence of the many detachments which
had gone out, consisting, as may be supposed,
of our strongest and healthiest men, and
commanded by our ablest battalion officers.
Still, though mustering scarcely 400 combat-

ants, the commandant put a bold face upon the matter. All the persons living on the southern side of the river were directed to cross, and to establish themselves and their baggage under the guns of the citadel. The hospitals were emptied of every man who might have strength enough to level a musket; and these being planted under cover of the palisades, were directed to maintain their post to the last extremity. At the same time the utmost care was taken to keep down a mutinous spirit, which the first rumour of an advance on the part of their countrymen had excited among the inhabitants. They were commanded by proclamation not to show themselves in the streets, and were told that wherever two should be found holding converse together they would certainly be shot. Every thing, indeed, was done, which in a very trying case courage could suggest, or prudence dictate; and the results were, that courage and prudence prevailed over mere numbers, to direct which there was mani-festly no head present.

Among other officers of merit my master chanced to be detached; and with me it mainly rested to save his property from the danger of confiscation. I was established in a house close to one of the barricades, where, up to this moment, the people had been particularly civil; but now, when I came to pack up and made preparations for moving, their tone entirely changed. They refused to lend a helping hand in any way; and not only rejected my application for a skin of wine, but told me with significant looks, that of wine I should not much longer stand in need. Such conduct of course served only to irritate; and I was forced to use the show of violence, by levelling a pis-tol at the padrone's head; but there was no occasion to go farther. I got my mules and horses laden; and securing about two gal-lons of wine, retired, with my fellow-servants, to the heights near the castle, whence we commanded an excellent view of the Spanish bivouac. Why did they not push on? Why did they halt, out of musket-shot of the palisades, and make there an idle display of their numbers? They ought to have known their enemies better than to suppose that they were the sort of people to be over-awed by any thing of the sort. Had they made the attempt, bravely, resolutely, and without a check, it must have proved successful. How earnestly I wished that half the number of English troops had been there; for the booty would have been pro-digious; all the treasures, with no inconsi-derable portion of the stores of the whole French army, being, by some strange over-sight, kept, not in the castle, but in the town.

The Spaniards either did not know this, or they held the garrison in too much re-spect; for they contented themselves with driving in, towards dusk, a solitary advanced post, and taking possession of the convent within which it had been established. We saw them then light their fires, and make preparations as if to invest the place, and try upon it the tedious process of a siege. But even to this plan, absurd enough it must be admitted, they failed to adhere. Throughout two days the blockade, such as it was continued. They were days to us of very considerable discomfort; for we knew our own weakness, and scarcely dared to hope that it was hidden from them: yet they came to an end at last, and with them all fears respecting the issue. The dawn of the third morning showed the Spanish lines abandoued. Not a man remained beside the fires, which had been recently trimmed and continued to burn, nor was so much as a dog left behind. Yet the Spaniards had not retreated in the proper sense of that term. Intelligence of the routes pursued by our various detachments having reached them, they broke up into parties, and hurried off, with the view of intercepting these on the march, and so winning both glory and riches from the spoil with which they were known to be laden.   They succeeded, however, very imperfectly in both objects.   Several of our detachments sustained, indeed, a heavy loss; and one, which, when it went abroad, consisted of a hundred men, returned with no more than fifty; but not in a solitary instance was the escort overpowered, or the booty taken away of which it was in charge.

It is marvellous even now to think of the extreme accuracy with which the Spaniards were accustomed to inform themselves, not only of the movements of the French troops, but of the personal habits and circumstances of the individuals by whom detached bodies were commanded.   On the present occasion, for example, there was a French lieutenant-colonel sent forth with a hundred infantry in a particular direction: he was a brave and a skilful officer, and though attacked by an overwhelming force of cavalry, he repulsed them twenty times at least, keeping his treasure always in the centre of his square. But he was known to the assailants as one who never stirred abroad without carrying all his private property in a sort of valise behind him, so that, while advancing to charge, the Spaniards would call out to him that they were determined to have his doubloons, and that he had better give them up quietly. The Frenchman held his course undaunted, and had wellnigh reached Burgos ere the fatal bullet struck him. But he died at last, from a pistol-shot in the head; and his valise, containing about a hundred-and-fifty gold pieces, became the property of the brave men who had, for twelve long hours, sustained his honour and their own in a very unequal contest.

For some time after the occurrence of these events, my master and I kept our station in

Burgos. He, like others, had lost a good many men from his detachment, and one officer, whose poodle dog attached itself to me; but he had received no wound himself, and, though still delicate, was able, for a while at least, to go through with his duties. I am not sure, however, that my readers would be very deeply interested were I to detail to them the manner in which day after day was spent; let me be content, therefore, to repeat one or two anecdotes, as illustrating the sort of life which at that period I led, and then we will pass together into new scenes, some of which may possibly offer to them greater attractions than the mere transcript of a prisoner's diary.

I was one day crossing the bridge at Burgos, when, to my great surprise, I encountered a man dressed in the uniform of the 12th English Light Dragoons. We entered, as may be imagined, at once into conversation, and I ascertained that he had been taken at

Grenalda; that he was a farrier by trade, and then in the service of the French General, Count d'Orsun. A very extraordinary fellow was my friend, Richard Kilby; his ingenuity as a working smith surpassed all that I have ever witnessed, and, as a horse doctor, he had either great skill or great good luck; but he was a determined drunkard—a profound hater of the French nation—and, beyond compare, the most self-willed and obstinate individual of his race. He and I became, as a matter of course, sworn allies: we were much together, for I helped him to turn his shoes; and, acting as his interpreter, I first procured for him from his master those supplies of money without which his genius never could have found a channel in which to exercise itself ; yet I more than once had reason to regret that an intimacy was ever struck up between us, and am forced, though reluctantly, to acknowledge that, when our destinies carried us in different directions, I

shed no tears over the prospect of being separated from him for ever.

My friend Richard hated the French, and
never omitted an opportunity of telling them
so: to be sure, he could not speak one word
of their language, nor did they understand a
syllable of his, so that the pleasant epithets
of " coward," " scoundrel," " rogue," " thief,"
with which it was his constant practice to
greet them, passed by unnoticed, because
unknown. But in more ways than this he
delighted to tease them, and he was quite
indefatigable in indulging his humours. For
example, his style of shoeing was so univer-
sally. and justly admired that there was no
end to the applications which were made to
him by the French officers. He would never
attend to them, except when the purse was
at the lowest ebb, and even then he took
care to insult the groom by holding the
charger tight with one hand, and so keeping
him, till the amount of the charge—eight

francs—was put into the other. He was constantly involving himself in quarrels, from the ruinous consequences of which nothing short of his master's rank in the service could have saved him; and once, at least, even that might have failed, but for the peculiar prowess by which he opposed, and finally repulsed, the assailants. The story is this:

One Sunday, Richard and I strolled beyond the limits of the town, and entering a wine-house, drank our bottle of Malaga, on the conclusion of which Richard complained of being hungry. The woman of the house was cleaning, at the moment, a number of salt herrings, two of which Richard secured, and put upon the coals to broil. He had not perceived that some French grenadiers, who equally with ourselves chanced to be inmates of the apartment, had likewise made a purchase of herrings, and were dressing them; and, having occasion to go out for a moment, he was rendered quite furious by meeting one of these men with a couple of herrings in his hand. Richard swore that the fish were his—wrested them from the grenadier, abused him like a pickpocket, and stripping off his jacket, challenged the Frenchman to fight. Now, the Frenchman, must have stood at least six feet three from the ground, whereas the extreme height of Richard could not exceed five feet; yet there was the little farrier squaring at the giant, and so conducting himself that the latter, in absolute amazement, became rooted to the spot. The landlady, in great alarm, entreated me to withdraw my friend, and, with some difficulty, I succeeded in doing so; but it was only that he might thrust himself into another situation, to the full as perilous, and far more laughable, than this. We adjourned to an old haunt of Richard's—to the house of a woman whom he had dubbed his mother; and who, being regularly put in possession of the whole amount of his earnings, could not refuse—even though it was the hour of Divine service—to open her door to her son. Accordingly, we entered, were shown into a parlour up stairs, and earnestly besought to keep quiet, otherwise the landlady must get into a scrape.

We sat quietly enough, till Dick observed a patrol of gendarmes ascending the street, and approaching the site of his mother's dwelling. His wrath against their nation was kindled, and he began first to swear and then to sing at the top of his lungs. They halted before the door, and ordered him to be quiet, but he only sang the louder. Then they knocked and tried to enter, but the door was bolted, and Dick hastened to reinforce the bolts by piling up furniture against it. The gendarmes threatened and blustered, while Dick, finding in one corner of the room a bag of large onions, opened upon them, with these strange missiles, a heavy fire. As might be expected, they were furious, and though he kept them somewhat at bay as long as his ammunition lasted, they would have certainly forced an entrance in the end, had he not plied them with water—not scalding hot, certainly, yet neither very cool, nor in its nature very limpid. The guard retreated with precipitation before such a torrent, and Richard shouted and laughed, as they shook their ears—for his supply had been both copious and very liberally dispensed.

Not having any particular desire to connect my own name with pranks of this sort, I escaped from Richard as soon as the coast was clear, and scarcely saw him again till within a day or two of our final separation; though I heard of him from time to time, and always heard with sorrow, that he continued to be the same reckless and unhappy man that he was when I first encountered him. Neither was his end unworthy of the earlier part of his career. Having accompanied his master to Pampeluna, and wellnigh exhausted his patience, Dick, in a drunken fit, deserted; and falling among the guerillas, was by them passed on from station to station, till he finally rejoined his regiment in Portugal. But he came with a constitution entirely undermined: against the excessive hardships which he encountered with the guerillas, a frame worn down by hard drinking, could not hold up; and within a few days after having reported himself to the adjutant, he expired. Richard left a son, like himself a farrier, who afterwards served with me on the cavalry staff, and many a day have we spent hours together in mutually detailing, one to another, anecdotes of his father's eccentricities.

I do not remember that there occurred any thing else of moment while I continued in Burgos, unless, indeed, the purchase of an Irish horse may be so regarded, which, when led in by a French groom, in a very miserable state, I instantly recognised as having once belonged to one of my troop-mates in the 11th. He was so savage a brute that neither his new master nor his servants could ride him; for a French officer had purchased him of an Englishman, in Portugal, for ten Napoleons, and the Count Golstein got him, in consequence, for the same sum that had been paid for him. But the horse knew me immediately: when I called him by his name, he turned his head and snuffed me all over, and became in my hands as quiet and tractable as a lamb. With none else, indeed, would he condescend to be familiar,—for even my master never rode him but once; but he followed me like a dog, and neighed and whinnied whenever he heard my voice even at a distance. The count gave him to me, and I rode him constantly for two years; at the termination of which, his vicious humours wore out, so that the count's son, to whom I ultimately transferred him, found him invaluable as a charger, and received the most satisfactory proofs of his hardihood. *Musch,* as he was called, carried the young Count Golstein through the whole of the campaign to Moscow and the retreat in which it ended; and, though much reduced in flesh, was still in excellent health when he came again under my care in his master's stables.

CHAPTER XII.

We return to France.

AFTER a residence in Burgos of something more than two months, the Count Golstein received permission to revisit his native country. He was accordingly directed to proceed to Vittoria, and join himself there to the sort of caravan which year by year passed, under a strong escort, through the dangerous defiles of the Pyrenees into France. I went with him, of course, and never enjoyed myself more, in every sense of the term, than during the week or two which, while waiting for the assembling of the party, we spent in the capital of the Basque provinces. Vittoria is a singularly pleasant place,—for a Spanish town clean and tidy, and well regulated; and, being built along the side of a hill, is very healthy, besides being abundantly supplied with pure and excellent water. It struck me, also, that the people were more alive to the influences of climate than those of the more fertile plains of Castile and Arragon. The women, in particular, were both beautiful in point of feature, and singularly graceful, as well in their attire as in their movements; and the humbler classes came too near, in their habits, to what we read of the damsels of old Palestine and Greece, not to be in my eyes objects of peculiar interest. Like the orientals, they go to draw water at the public fountain; and the vases in which they carry home the pure element are at once strictly classical in their shape, and poised, with classical exactness, on the heads of the bearers. It used to excite both our surprise and interest to see with what unerring exactitude they bore their pitchers from the well to their own houses. There was no balancing the instrument by means of the hand. Planted upon the top of the head, it appeared to rest there by virtue of some balancing power inherent in the bearer; and over the roughest ground, as surely as over the smoothest, she passed without spilling a drop. I cannot tell how often I have been tempted to stand by and admire these beautiful "drawers of water," and if from time to time I was tempted to carry on with one or another a little innocent flirtation, I pray the more rigid of my readers not to judge me too harshly for the act of imprudence.

If any thing could have taught the French that their chances of reducing Spain to obedience were blank, the care which they were obliged to exercise for the purpose of passing the most ordinary convoy across the border ought to have done so. I believe that there was no instance on record of a moderately-sized party attempting that passage, and saving so much as an individual alive, to tell how it had fared with his companions. And even the accumulations of months, though escorted by a strong battalion, were glad by all manner of disguises to conceal the true moment of their starting. I found, for example, that, inclusive of sick, wounded, weary, and persons whom real business drew out of Spain, not fewer than 10,000 people were, when I reached Vittoria, assembled there, for the single purpose of being passed, under a military guard, into France. Moreover, a corps of 600 infantry, with four fieldpieces, were appointed to guard them; and of waggons laden with baggage, and public and private plunder, there was no end. Yet, multitudinous as we were, it was not accounted safe to undertake the threading of those dangerous defiles, except under the protection of a stratagem. Thus there came out an order from the commandant, warning the travellers that, at a certain hour in

the morning of the third day subsequently
to the issue of his proclamation, they should
be ready to begin their journey. As might
be expected, intelligence of this arrangement spread far and wide through the provinces, and, without doubt, the guerillas
were everywhere on the alert, to intercept
and profit by the movement. But we stole
a march upon them. On the day immediately succeeding that on which the gover-
nor's handbill took its place at the corners
of the streets, there appeared a supple-
mentary command, by which we were directed to pack our baggage, and hold ourselves in readiness to move in one hour.

Never was the wisdom of any arrangement more distinctly proved than this. We
had scarcely cleared the outskirts of the
town, ere groups of brigands began to draw
near us, which seemed to accumulate
strength in proportion as we penetrated
deeper and deeper among the mountains.

But they never acquired such a power of numbers as to justify them in their own eyes in making a serious attack; and we, in consequence, suffered nothing from first to last except from an occasional and very desultory fire of musketry. At the same time there was enough, in the whole progress of the journey, to divert my attention for the moment, and to make a deep impression upon my memory. In the first place, the scenery exceeded, in point of grandeur, all through which I had previously passed. So bold, indeed, were the ascents, and so steep the paths by which we regained the depths of the valleys, that over and over again I used to wonder how cars, and waggons, and even horses, contrived to traverse them. And then the wood was gorgeous in the extreme: the magnificent cork-tree overshadowing the base of mountains,—on the sides, and here and there the brows, of which waved far and

wide whole forests of oak, and pine, and hazel.
But that which gave to our journey its most
engrossing interest was the constant proximity
of bands of robbers, who, like the vultures
that hover over a battle-field, seemed to
track our course, and seize every opportunity that offered of molesting us. Repeatedly
were we fired upon from the summits of in-
accessible corries, and repeatedly threatened
with more serious interruptions, which,
however, our great numerical superiority,
aided by the excellency of the device which
had hindered them from assembling in force
enough to meet us, effectually prevented.
Yet the knowledge that danger was constantly at hand failed not to produce its effects as well upon the imaginative as upon
the timid. And, finally, the bracing nature of the climate operated upon our nerves
and spirits to an extent which I have no
language adequate to describe. But the
case may be judged of so soon as I state, that

when, towards sunset on the second day, we
arrived in sight of Irun, there were comparatively few among us who did not experience a sensation not very far from regret
that their perils were surmounted.

If I felt sorry at first on finding that I had
quitted the salubrious air of the mountains,
the feeling was at once dispelled when, to
my great surprise, I found myself addressed,
just after entering the town, by one who
spoke to me in excellent English, and whom,
in spite of the total change in his style and
attire, I soon recognised as a former comrade in the 11th. I think that I have elsewhere spoken of one Nicholas Brown, an
American by birth, who served in my
own troop, and whose liberation from the
prison at Salamanca I had been the means
of procuring. But, however this may be,
the person who now addressed me proved
to be this same Brown, and the reception
which he gave me was not more creditable

to himself than it was, in the highest degree, acceptable to me. I confess that, when
we first encountered, I was a good deal surprised by the elegance of his attire and
bearing. Neither was the sentiment di-
minished when he conducted me to his
apartments,—three well-furnished rooms in
the commandant's house,—and, ringing the
bell, ordered a servant to provide all things
necessary for our recreation. So, also, the
display of his wardrobe, his jewellery, and,
though last not least, his ready money, im-
pressed me with sentiments of great respect.
But when the truth came out, my surprise,
at least, suffered a remarkable diminution.
The commandant's lady—not his wife—had,
it appeared, taken a fancy to Brown. She
was young, beautiful, and extremely fasci-
nating; and Brown, acting as men in his
circumstances are apt to do, readily gave
himself up to the bright intoxication. All
his wishes were in consequence prevented;

and he very fairly told me, that, let him escape from the condition of a prisoner when he might, he would certainly not rejoin his regiment. I confess that, bearing the fact in my mind, that he was not an Englishman by lineage, I scarcely blamed him for this; but, even if I had, the fact of his meditating a public wrong to the state would have scarcely justified me, in my own eyes, for rejecting his private kindness. I spent a day with him very pleasantly; and, next morning, when we marched, as we did at five o'clock, he rode several miles in my company; neither did we part without feelings of sincere and mutual regret.

We halted for a couple of days in Bayonne, of the position and capabilites of which it is not necessary for me to say any thing. The intrenched camp, which at a later stage in the war covered and rested upon it, was not then begun; neither were the sluices taken up, nor the low ground flooded; but the permanent fortifications both of the town and the citadel were in excellent order; and being a sort of depot station for most of the regiments employed in the north and east of Spain, it could boast of a strong, if not a very homogeneous garrison. It is cut in halves, as the reader doubtless knows, by the river Adour; and can boast of a population greater by far, than the surface extent of the site would lead the traveller to imagine. But I cannot say that my remembrances of Bayonne are very agreeable; so I content myself with stating, that we turned our backs upon it with little regret; and plunging into that strange and wild district called the Llandes, passed on by way of Dax, towards Bordeaux.

The Llandes have been too often and too accurately described by other travellers, to render so much as an allusion to the peculiarity of the scenery admissible from me. It is an enormous plain of sand, which extends along the sea from Bayonne to Bordeaux, and measures, at a moderate computation, at least two hundred miles in length, by fifty or sixty, or perhaps more, in breadth. In ancient times, the sands used to be quite bare, and to shift, like those of the desert of Alexandria, with every high wind that blew, till a pious monk—whose name I heard, but have forgotten — showed his countryman how to reclaim, by planting the waste with pine-trees. The roots of the pine served as braces to bind the sand together. The leaves and cones, as they fell and decayed, created a soil; and now we come, from time to time, in traversing a huge forest, upon extensive clearances, over which flocks of sheep and herds of cattle wander, and neat villages are scattered. It struck me, also, that the inhabitants of the Llandes were a very happy, as well as a primitive race. They seemed to have every thing about them in abundance, which is necessary to sustain life, and many articles of simple luxury. Moreover, they were light of heart, free of speech, bold hunters of the wolf and of the bear; and, as I could gather as much from what I saw as what I heard, daring smugglers. Yet they appeared to be an innocent race, notwithstanding this latter propensity; and their deference for their priests was worthy of the patriarchal times. Many a pleasant dance I had with the young women, and many a pleasant chat with the old, after our tents were pitched, and our horses dressed, and our convoy established.

We traversed the Llandes in the space, if I recollect right, of five days, having been greatly interested throughout the journey, as well with the nature of the country, as with the happy condition of its inhabitants. Our resting-place was Bordeaux, of which, for the same reasons which held me back from describing Bayonne, I do not think that it is worth while to say any thing. It is a noble city, very clean, full of bustle, and adorned with many gorgeous edifices; and enriched as well as beautified by the proximity of the Garonne, which, in a fine volume of water, flows past it. Besides, the opportunities afforded me of minutely examining the place were not great; for my master having brought with him certain relics of a French general who had been a friend of his, and fallen in battle, set out, on the day after our arrival, for the château in which the widow dwelt, that he might tell her how her husband's last moments were spent, and hand over to her his treasures. I dare say, that to the poor bereaved lady the visit was sad enough, for she was a young and delicate creature, not more, as it seemed, than twenty-five years of age; and her countenance, when I saw her, told a tale of hopes altogether blighted. But to me the excursion was full of interest, and therefore I may as well make mention of it.

The château towards which our steps
were turned, lay a good day's journey from
Bordeaux; and to reach it, we passed
through a succession of vineyards, inter-
spersed with luxuriant groves of olive and
myrtle. The highest order of cultivation,
too, was present everywhere, and food for
ourselves, as well as forage for our horses,
was both cheap and abundant. But it was
the abode of the widow and her domestic
establishment that principally engaged my
attention; for any thing more gorgeous, yet
peculiar, I never witnessed. We reached a
village towards dusk, at the bottom of which
stood the château,—a fine mansion, with extensive stables and outhouses attached,—and
our reception, so soon as my master's name
had been announced, was of the most gratifying kind. The entire household seemed,
indeed, to greet our arrival as a jubilee. My
master was led at once into the presence of
the lady; while I had the horses taken from

me, and was conducted into a room, where a dozen maids were assembled, and seated forthwith as the honoured guest among them. Not one word of their language could I speak, nor one in a dozen could I understand; and as for my efforts, whether I addressed them in English, or Spanish or German, they were alike unprofitable to gain a hearing. Yet we continued to converse, amid a great deal of laughter, by signs; and as to drinking healths, that was managed by hob-nobbing our glasses at momentary intervals. It was, upon the whole, the most amusing meal that I ever ate; and the viands, as well as the wines, were excellent.

We spent two days with the French general's widow, throughout which we were treated with the greatest possible kindness. My master was sumptuously lodged, in an apartment the walls of which were entirely covered with mirrors, and the floor laid with oak, on which the polish was so fine that, till I pulled off my boots, I at least could not stand upon it without slipping. There was, too, a peculiarity about that chamber, which, on one occasion put me to some inconvenience. The door shut with a spring; and being, like the panels, overlaid with glass, I found it impossible to make my way out again, till my master, waking from his first sleep, put his hand upon the catch and threw it open. As to my own billet, it was extremely comfortable, though in a remote and gloomy wing of the castle. And then the grounds were perfectly beautiful, with parterres of flowers, terraces rising above one another, all in the formal order of the French school. But it is not worth while to continue these details any further. We abode in this hospitable mansion till the morning of the third day; on the arrival of, which we bade our friends farewell, and returned the same evening to Bordeaux.

CHAPTER XIII.

I pursue my Journey—Domestic Brawl—A Sutler—
Germany—Dusseldorf—Changes of Fortune.

OUR march from Bordeaux carried us
by easy stages through a very beautiful
country, the whole surface of which was covered with vine plantations. We halted,
likewise, for one night in a large town, of
which I have forgotten the name, but which,
from its general aspect, and the business in
which the inhabitants were engaged, re-
minded me very much of Birmingham. By-
and-by we reached Orleans, still famous for
its statue of Joan of Arc in the market-
place, and well filled, at the period of which
I now speak, with English detenus. I can-

not, however, pretend to give any description
of a city in which my sojourn extended not
beyond a single day; nor, which was at the
moment still more mortifying to myself, did
I on that occasion visit Paris at all. For,
though the count had gone before us to the
capital, his instructions to us were, that we
should turn short by the road to the Rhenish
provinces, without touching on the great
city; and we, albeit sorely mortified at the
circumstance, had no choice except to obey.
Accordingly, we journeyed on, leisurely and
very pleasantly, through a rich country, and
under the influence of a genial sun ; taking
care to halt, whenever the opportunity offered, at some pleasant village for the night,
and always meeting from the villagers a very
friendly reception.

We (I mean the count's domestics and
baggage) were attended throughout the
march by a small escort of Polish dragoons.
I mention this fact, because the wife of one

of the party acted as a sort of sutler to the cavalcade, and by the oddity of her appearance, as well as the strangeness of her proceedings, was the occasion of a good deal of merriment and some wonder. She was singularly short, and happened to be in a state when women in general avoid horse exercise. Yet there she was, day after day, mounted cross-legged on a brute at least seventeen hands high, and laden with eggs, bottles, and glasses, out of which she dispensed, with a liberal hand, Cognac to such as required it. One day we missed her from her accustomed place. The cavalcade set forward, and she went not with it; ay, and more extraordinary still, when the halting hour came, the Circular Pole, as we called her, failed to make her appearance; so we were forced to get our schnaps, sorely against our will, at the auberge. In like manner the march of the following day began, without restoring us to our Hebe; and something like anxiety was rising among us, when all at once there was seen in the rear a tall horse at a swinging trot, and a human form, or else that of a baboon, perched upon its back. The question of humanity did not, however, remain unsolved long after the apparition arrived within ear-shot; for the old cry, " Boir, boir, monsieurs, ein glass brande-wine," soon told us that our old friend was still in the land of the living. Nor did she come alone: strapped upon her back, like a bundle of rags, was a thumping boy, which in the stable of the last halting-place had first seen the light ; and which, as well as its mother, showed that it was sound in wind, whatever might be the case as to limbs. I confess that I was astounded; yet what will not Nature do when circumstances make extraordinary demands on her?

In this manner we passed.the fortresses of Cambray, Valenciennes, and Avesnes, at the latter of which my fellow-servants and I came

to an open rupture. They had never for-
given me the favour which our common master showed me, and here they made up their
minds to let me feel the extent of their
vengeance. It happened, either by accident
or design, that the coachman, after washing
the carriage, placed it exactly across my stable
door, so that I could neither get access to the
horses nor lead them out to water. I could
not suppose that there was design in the
matter, neither did I care to put his good
humour to the test by begging him to remove
it; so I wheeled it on one side with my own.
hands, and proceeded to arrange the horses.
My work was yet incomplete, when forth
from the house rushed my comrades: the
valet took the lead, and a volley of abuse was
instantly heaped upon me. At first I kept
my temper wonderfully. I asked them what
was wrong, and received in reply only fresh
abuse; till, by-and-by, my anger was in its
turn kindled, and I told the valet that, if he

were not an old man, I would wring his nose from his face. " Would you ?" cried he, " we'll see." So saying, he ran aside, armed himself with a sword, and advanced towards me in a menacing attitude. I was very much irritated, dashed into the stable, got a good broom-handle, and rushing out, prepared to do battle; but lo! my enemy was gone. I searched for him everywhere, but in vain; till at last a thought striking me that he might have ensconced himself in the carriage, I wrenched open one of the doors, and he leaped out through the other. Away he ran across a meadow, still carrying with him the naked sword, and away I set in pursuit; till, coming up with him, I knocked the weapon out of his hand, and laid him sprawling on the grass. He now cried for quarter, and I gave it; as, indeed, after soundly rating them all, I extended my forgiveness to the rest of the household; and it is but fair to add, that, having amply apologised, and promised better

behaviour in the time to come, they conducted themselves towards me ever afterwards with the greatest good feeling and
attention.

We did not enter Paris, but leaving it
on one side, took the road by Liège, and
through Brabant, towards Aix-la-Chapelle.
It seemed to me as if a perpetual carnival
were established. The villages, as we traversed them, were all alive with the gaieties and dissipations of a fair; and strange
to say, the occurrence of each festival
seemed to keep pace with our arrival at
the scene of the merry-making. I was
greatly pleased with all that I saw, and enjoyed both the bustle of Liège, where there
are extensive iron-works, and the monastic
gravity of Aix-la-Chapelle, where Napoleon's
mother kept, in my day, a species of court,
and divided with the tomb of Charlemagne
the notice of strangers. The people did not

speak in very favourable terms of her whom they described as the empress-mother. On the contrary, they represented her to be avaricious in the extreme; so much so, indeed, as to visit the market in person, and cheapen the articles that might be needed for her own household consumption.* But the circumstance which most of all gave to Aix-la-Chapelle its claims upon my notice was, that here the count, who had rejoined us near Paris, met, for the first time after three years' absence, his wife and family. And a very joyful greeting it was; for the countess came, with her two daughters and her sister, to welcome her lord to his home, and

* The Light Dragoon's observations agree in every respect with what higher and better authority has told us. Napoleon's mother was very stingy; yet there was a spirit of rationalism in it too. " You wish me to spend more money," was her answer to many who complained. " No, I will not. I shall have all these kings (meaning her sons) to support yet."

a happier group it has seldom been my fortune to witness in any part of the world.

We spent a couple of days at Aix-la-Chapelle, in order that the count and the countess might, according to etiquette, pay their respects to the empress-mother; after which we proceeded to Brael—for such was the name of my master's château, and of the grounds attached to it. The former was a baronial castle, moated and drawbridged as in ancient times, of prodigious extent, and confronted by stabling and coach-houses, where a hundred horses with a dozen of carriages might have been bestowed. The farm-yard was also capacious, and contained draught horses, cows, bulls, pigs, poultry, and all the usual appliances of a country-house, in abundance. So also the gardens, the orchards, and the woods were extensive; yet over the whole hung an air of neglect and desolation, such as bespoke a family in

decay, or suffering from extreme mismanage-
ment in its affairs.   I have reason to believe
that to the latter cause, rather than to the
encroachments of time or public calamity,
the dilapidated condition of Brael was owing;
for the late count had, it appeared, nomi-
nated his widow to be the guardian of the
property during his son's absence; and the
widow, being a woman of very irregular
habits, cruelly abused the trust.   The consequence was, that, when making a tour of
the castle, I found myself wandering from
one unfurnished room to another; the very
pictures themselves having been removed
from the walls and sold, in order that means
might be provided for the indulgence of her
passion for gaming.   I never shall forget the
expression of the count's face when this
scene of waste and desolation opened upon
him.   Not even the consciousness that he was
again in the bosom of his family seemed for
a while to afford him any relief: indeed, I

was half tempted to wonder that he did not apply to be sent back to his regiment, that, in the excitement and hurry of active service, his private mortifications might be forgotten.

The count was too little satisfied with his dilapidated and unfurnished castle to make there any lengthened stay; yet a strong sense of duty urged him to visit his mother, who dwelt in another château, likewise his property, at the distance of five leagues from Brael. It was called Bolingdorf; and thither, at the expiration of a few days, we proceeded. The old lady, eccentric in the extreme, gave us but a cool reception. We abode with her, nevertheless, upwards of a week, and greatly delighted the peasants and retainers by our display both of pomp and liberality: for the count, arraying his domestics in new liveries, rode to church in state, and gave a grand supper, to which a ball succeeded, in the largest of the barns that adjoined the mansion. Going to church in state, however, much more feasting the lowly on costly viands were not at all in the countess's way; so she and her son were not slow in discovering that one house would be too small to contain them both. Wherefore our family removed to my master's town-house in Dusseldorf; and there, not unpleasantly, about a year of my existence was spent.

Having now exchanged the condition of a soldier for that of a domestic in a private family, my readers will probably agree with me in opinion, that our wisest course will be, not to adhere any longer to the form of a connected narrative, but simply to describe such occurrences as from to time to time befel—to which at the moment some measure of interest was attached, and of which the remembrance is still cherished. Let me, then, begin by stating that the year which I spent in the neighbourhood of the Rhine was

that which witnessed the infliction of the
first great blow upon the colossal empire of
Napoleon. The Russian campaign was
begun, and the drain of men and horses, not
upon France alone, but upon all the States
subject to French influence, was terrible.
Among other districts, the duchy of Berg,
of which Dusseldorf is the capital, received
orders, early in 1813, to supply the grand
army with a reinforcement of five thousand
infantry and five hundred cavalry. Instantly
the conscription was called into play. Berg
had already been pretty well denuded of
the stoutest and most active of its youth;
but the present demand was peremptory,
and was carried out in total disregard of
mercy. Accordingly, the names of all the
male inhabitants between the ages of fif-
teen and fifty being already in the keeping of the proper authorities, a sort of
lottery-drawing took place, and forth from
the city went the gendarmes in every di-

rection to secure their prizes. It was shocking to see the poor wretches brought in,
twenty or thirty in a string, tied round the
neck with one cord, the end of which was
fastened to a mounted policeman's saddle.
And then for their lodging they had a parti-
cnlar barrack, being well and rigidly guarded
there by a body of old French soldiers, every
effort to corrupt whose fidelity proved as
fruitless as were the endeavours to elude or
deceive their vigilance. Once, and once only,
a band of conscripts contrived, by rising suddenly upon the guard, to break through the
barrier; of whom about two hundred effected
their escape; but even they, after wandering
some days in the woods, were glad to give
themselves up again; for the authorities having taken care to register each conscript as
he came in, noting down the exact name and
residence of his father and mother, the conscript himself became from that instant a
mere instrument in their hands. Had he

deserted, they did not care so much as to look for him; but they sent a patrol to his father's house, seized the old man, threw him into prison, and kept him there till his son came back to his standard. There was not one of all the two hundred fugitives who was not by these means recovered: for filial piety was in those days an active principle in Germany, nor was its power to influence the behaviour of individuals ever more clearly shown than in the case of which I am now speaking.

Such was the process by which five thousand men were, in the space of a few days, brought together. To collect the horses a device not less summary was adopted. Wherever the police agents saw within the duchy an animal which seemed to be fit for military service, they, without inquiring into its age or capabilities, seized it. The proprietor might complain, but who regarded him? He received, in compensation for the loss of his beast, an order upon the treasury for seven pounds sterling, which, in ninety-nine instances out of a hundred, proved to be worth its value in paper, and no more.

The men and horses being gathered together, the next thing was to officer and drill them; the former of which measures was carried out, at least in the cavalry, by breaking up the skeleton of a lancer regiment which had served in Spain, and distributing the troopers, as captains, lieutenants, and sub-lieutenants, throughout the newly-raised levy. With respect again to the infantry, I believe that an attempt was made to place them under the command of those of their own countrymen to whom in civil life they had been accustomed to look up; but it very imperfectly succeeded. Be this, however, as it may, three short weeks were all that could be granted for organizing and training the recruits; at the termination of which the whole were pronounced fit for service, and received the rout to march into Russia. Surely there never took the field such a body of cavalry; for the men were incapable of sitting their horses, and the horses unbroken to obey the bridle, far less the sound of the trumpet; and as to the infantry, they could prime and load, certainly, and fire, and load again; but of the evolutions of a common company's parade they knew nothing. Still the cry for men was great at headquarters, and the order was issued for the Bergers to march, after their officers should have presented themselves at a grand entertainment which General Travier, the individual appointed by the authorities at Paris to superintend the equipment of the levies in this quarter, had determined to give.

I was present at the dinner, my master, Count Golstein, having purposely desired me to wait upon himself; and a scene more perfectly ludicrous, more unlike to every thing of the sort which I had ever witnessed before, never, I must admit, passed under my observation. At the upper table, where sat General Travier, my master, the civil and military authorities of the place, and several men of rank from the neighbouring districts, matters went forward pretty much as at public dinners they are wont to do ; but among the gentry who crowded the long tables that stretched from one end of the hall to the other, a widely different state of things prevailed. There was scrambling and pushing while the viands were before them,—one was heaping an entire dish of vegetables on his plate, another seizing and keeping possession of a joint or a stew. This gallant captain upset a butter-boat in his neighbour's lap, — that newly-fledged lieutenant poured a jug of gravy over the shoulder of his friend beside him. It was everywhere " make sure of what you can reach, and never think of asking whether any body would like to share it with you."

And then, when the process of giving toasts began, surely no caricaturist, in the most extravagant flight of his fancy, ever imagined aught so grotesque. General Travier, to be sure, pledged the emperor with great spirit; and, though not one in twenty understood a word of what he said, was greeted, till he sat down, with cheers. Then followed " Success to the grand army," which was prefaced by an assurance that " the gentlemen whom he had the honour to address were fortunate men, inasmuch as they were about to march to certain glory, of which the fruits would be a speedy advancement to rank, distinctions, and wealth." That, too, was cheered, not least vociferously by those who could not comprehend a syllable of the argument which the eloquent speaker laboured to establish. But by-and-by wilder and louder words were heard. The gentlemen at the lower tables, conceiving that time was precious, helped themselves in bumpers,

and soon got drunk; whereupon the occu-
pants of the high table withdrew; and even
my disposition to laugh gradually exchanged
itself for a sense of deep disgust, and I,
though nowise required to do so, followed
my master.

Next morning, at seven o'clock, five thousand Berger infantry, and five hundred cavalry, began their march towards Russia.
It was a piteous spectacle that,—for wives,
and mothers, and sisters threw themselves
wildly into the ranks, and the sound of la-
mentation rose high above the notes of mar-
tial music. But what availed it? The de-
cree had gone forth,—the ill-fated conscripts
held their way,—and few, if any, ever returned to tell how it fared with them amid
the snows and frosts of Muscovy.

As the act of organizing this corps kept
Dusseldorf in a state of extreme bustle, so
the stillness that prevailed after the troops
had marched struck me as something awful.

You saw no human beings in the streets except women and children. Even the old men were few in number; for the conscription, like the standard of height, was often stretched; and they, like the women, seemed to be fairly bowed down with sorrow for the loss of their offspring. Every occurrence, therefore, which promised in any way to break in upon the gloom of total inaction was hailed, at least by me, as a relief; and two there did occur, very different in themselves to be sure, yet both so striking that I cannot think of passing them by unnoticed.

The first was the execution of a woman and her paramour for the murder of the husband of the former. The deceased had, it appeared, by frugality and ceaseless labour, contrived to amass some money as a maker of brooms, which brooms he was in the habit of cutting in a wood not far from the city. He, therefore, finding years increase upon him, hired a man to assist him, and his wife proceeded to form with that person an illicit connexion. They say that Love is blind, and, without all doubt, he showed himself, in this instance, to be at least fearfully short-sighted; for while the frail fair one was really a handsome woman, the gallant, if not absolutely deformed, was but by a hair-breadth removed from deformity. Nevertheless he had charms in the eyes of the broom-maker's wife, so irresistible, that at last it was agreed between them that the husband should be put out of the way.

The poor man was missed; but as his wife represented him to have gone on a visit to some relatives at a distance nobody inquired further, and for several weeks all went on smoothly. At the termination of this interval, however, a body was found, very much decomposed, yet distinguishable as that of the broom-maker, floating on the surface of a pond or small lake, which lay deep in the forest whence his besoms used to be drawn. It was immediately conveyed into the city, and the woman and her lover being arrested, arrangements were made for putting them on their trial. How closely does the eye of Providence watch over the life of man ; and how rarely are they who shed man's blood permitted to escape. Two children, the eldest only eleven years old, had, as it now came out, been spectators of the butchery. They saw the old man—for he was full sixty years of age—come, with his journeyman and his wife, to his accustomed spot, and stoop down, as he was wont to do, for the purpose of cutting the heather where it was longest. He was thus employed when his servant stole behind and felled him to the ground with a blow from a bludgeon. The blows were repeated till his victim ceased to struggle ; and then he, with his paramour, dragged the body to the edge of the pond and threw it in. But life, as it appeared, had not been extinguished ; for the guilty pair turning round, after they had

proceeded some way from the spot, beheld
their victim dragging himself towards the
shore, by means of the bulrushes which grew
in large quantities round the edges of the
pond.   Instantly the woman turned back,
and, seizing a broom-handle, she pushed her
husband back into the water, and held him
under till he expired.

These facts having been proved at the
trial, there could, of course, be no doubt as
to the nature of the sentence. Both criminals
were condemned to be guillotined; but as it
was necessary in those days to get the sentence of death confirmed at Paris, several
weeks elapsed ere the wretched pair were
taught that with them the business of the
world was ended.   The woman, I was assured, made very strenuous efforts to obtain,
if not a pardon, at least a commutation of her
sentence.   She offered to pay as much as ten
thousand dollars into the imperial treasury.
Yet the emperor, or his representatives,

though sorely pressed for the sinews of war,
refused, point blank, to have any dealings
with her. Accordingly the day was fixed,
and at the time appointed she and her part-
ner in crime were brought from the prison to
the scaffold, each in an open cart, and each
attended by a priest, who seemed, to do him
justice, most assiduous in the discharge of
his duty. The wretched woman looked to
her spiritual comforter with attention. Her
whole demeanour, likewise, was that of one
who knows that it is the reverse of a light
matter to die; whereas the man, either from
ignorance, or because he was more master of
himself, exhibited no symptoms at all of concern. Both were, however, firm; nor did
she, even when the executioner stripped her
to the waist, shrink from her doom. But I
must not go on. It is a horrible species of
punishment. Easy it may be to the delin-
quent, when compared with strangulation;
but on the spectator the effect is far more

disgusting: for there is something frightful in the literal shedding of blood, especially as by the guillotine it is shed—in torrents. Let me, then, be content to state, that in three seconds after they had been fastened to the machine they lay before us, successively, headless trunks; while we, or at least I, turned away, utterly sickened by the spectacle of which I had been the witness.

The second anecdote which I undertook to repeat has reference to a phenomenon on which, for aught I know to the contrary, may be founded the well-known legend which records the destruction of a tyrannical chief in his own castle, on the Rhine, by an inroad of rats. The country about Dusseldorf is subject to periodical visitations from myriads of field-mice. These tiny marauders advance in such numbers, that every effort to destroy them fails; and wherever they go they mow down the standing wheat before them, as surely and wellnigh as quickly, as a band of reapers. They feed entirely on the roots of the stalk; and, grubbing for their food, while the stalk is yet green, they utterly destroy as they go forward. Moreover, they can neither be arrested nor turned out of their direct route; but forward they go, like the hurricane, in a straight line, and their operations are scarcely than the hurricane less destructive. I tried to persuade the people that, if they would only dig a deep and wide trench across the field, the small marauders would be stopped; but they paid no attention to me. And the consequence was, that, throughout a space of several miles,—on a plateau not very wide, to be sure, but exceedingly fertile,—all the labours of the seed-time were rendered profitless, and the husbandmen entirely cheated of their harvest. At last the army of foragers reached a running stream, which they could not pass; and I believe that, in their efforts to do so, they all perished.

The people of Berg are very superstitious, and, in one sense of the phrase, extremely philosophical. No sooner were the mice gone, than they set about collecting the da= maged grain, laying it up as forage for the cattle during the winter. And, while they shrugged their shoulders, and declared that the visitation came from God, and could not, therefore, be avoided, they comforted them- selves by the anticipation of a crop, tenfold more abundant than that which had been lost, on the following autumn. I have rea- son to believe that the calculation in question never fails them. Whether it is that the mice manure the land as they go on, or that the removal of the grain by the process of mining spares the soil more than if it were reaped, I cannot pretend to say; but experience has shown, that the season immediately succeed- ing that of a visitation of the sort is invariably more prolific, by many degrees, than the sea- sons usually are. So bountiful is nature in all her arrangements, even when she seems at times to have declared war against us.

Time passed; and each new week—I might have said each new day—beheld detachment after detachment arrive from the interior of France, halt to organize itself, and provide horses for the conveyance of its baggage, and then push on, as the event proved, to certain destruction. Every animal that could move or carry a load, be it ever so trifling, was, of course, taken up, and my kind master, among others, parted with all his stud, leaving me, for the first time since I joined him, entirely destitute of employment. It was under these circumstances, and with his entire approbation, that I consented to transfer my services to an English family, called Grainger, then resident in the place, and with them for a while I lived in great comfort, albeit certainly not in idleness. But the crisis had come, on which, at a period not remote, he would have been accounted

insane who should have reckoned; and bands
of stragglers, making their way back to their
homes, told us of the entire overthrow of
the grand army. The battle of Leipsic was
fought; and the wreck of the combatants
might, it appeared, be expected in full retreat
for the Rhine, which they desired to inter-
pose between themselves and their pursuers.
Moreover, the vigilance of the French in
guarding their prisoners, as well on the German as on the opposite side of the river, seemed
to relax; and, one after another, the captives
regained their freedom, though not without
the endurance of much suffering. I remember
one bitter cold day, in the depth of the winter
of 1813-14, going out early in the morning
for the purpose of washing the carriage, and
encountering at the yard-gate a spectacle
which greatly interested me. It was a young
man, dripping with wet, from whose person
the icicles were hanging, and who earnestly
besought me to tell whether there was not

an Englishman in the place. After a little discussion, I made myself known, and learned that he, a countryman of my own, with three others, had escaped from a depot of prisoners on the other side, and, swimming the Rhine, were now all but dead from cold, having crouched together throughout the night in a gravel-pit. I took them in, as may be supposed, carried them to the servants' hall, lighted a good fire in the stove, and from my own wardrobe supplied them with a change of dress. My master likewise behaved to them with great kindness; and, concealing them for a while, we eventually contrived to pass them on, by a route which secured to them a good chance of reaching England in safety. They had, it appeared, been mates of merchant-vessels, in which capacity they were taken; and the name of one was Robinson, from Tooley-street, in the Borough. I cannot recall to my remembrance the precise channel through which intelligence of

their safe return to London reached me; yet
I know that they did escape in a smuggler
from Holland.   I hope that they have since
prospered.

The Englishmen were scarcely gone, when
evidences, more and more conclusive, of the
turn which affairs had taken at Napoleon's
head-quarters, began everywhere to exhibit
themselves.   Rumour after rumour came in
of fresh disasters sustained, and of a universal
disposition, exhibiting itself throughout the
whole of the Rhenish provinces, to rise
against the iron yoke under which they had
so long lain.   The people, indeed, were
everywhere eager to be led against their
oppressors; but chiefs to direct the insur-
rection, were wanting, and the consequence was, that an outbreak which occurred at Elberfeldt was put down, with
great loss to the insurgents.   It was determined, also, by the victors to make an example of four of the ringleaders, by putting

them publicly to death in the four most po-
pulous towns in the district; and one, an
unfortunate weaver, was brought to Dusseldorf, that he might there undergo the sentence which a court-martial had awarded.
I went to the great square, for the purpose
of witnessing his execution; and a very
shocking sight it was. The poor man, who
had been wounded in the battle, was carried
upon a sort of litter, by four French grenadiers, and laid down in the market-place,
scarcely if at all conscious of what was
going on. A coffin had already been prepared for him, and he was thrown on the
ground beside it; in which attitude he was
shot, I verily believe, after the breath had
gone forth from the body. Neither this bar-
barous act, however, nor many more of a like
nature, sufficed to stem the tide of events,
which swept irresistibly onwards. The period of French domination was come, and

the lapse of a few days made all parties, whether friends or foes, aware of the fact.

While I was looking, like all around me, for what each new day might bring forth, I chanced, once upon a time, to pass through the market-place, where I encountered a man leading a mule by the halter, whom I felt myself irresistibly compelled to examine closely. My surprise may be imagined, when I recognised, in the squalid object before me, the same Joseph, who, on my first capture in Spain, had behaved to me with so much kindness. He had, it appeared, followed his master all the way to Moscow, and shared in the hardships of the subsequent retreat, at some stage in which the General was wounded, and sent on, with others in a similar plight, to France. Joseph, however, did not accompany him, but marched with his mule, throughout that inclement season, which cost the invaders of Russia so many lives, and utterly destroyed the French army. I took him to my home, of course, and strongly urged his making his way to England through Holland; but he refused to act on my advice. " The mule is loaded with my master's property," said he, " and I cannot bear the thought of wronging him of one fragment of it. I will take my chance, penetrate into France, and, having delivered it up, return home as I best can." There was no blaming him for acting on a principle of such perfect honesty, so I contented myself with giving him a share of my worldly goods, and recommending him to keep well ahead of the retreating army, I saw him to the edge of the Rhine, and there took leave of him.

I had just parted from Joseph, when I learned from some market-people that a corps of French troops was in full march towards the town. About noon they arrived, some six or seven hundred in num-

ber, bringing with them two eight-pounders
and a howitzer. They encamped outside
the barrier, whither, with many more, I
went to see them. Never have I beheld
troops in such a pitiable plight. Their
arms, I believe, were serviceable enough,
but their clothes were all in tatters; and
their frames, emaciated from constant fatigue, and the absence of regularity in their
diet, seemed altogether unequal to any further exertion. Their *morale*, likewise, appeared to be affected almost in an equal
degree with their physical powers, for the
very name of a Cossack made them shudder, and they were evidently incapable of
showing any steady front, if attacked. Nor,
indeed, was it intended that they should
attempt a stand on this side of the Rhine,
the object of their movement on Dusseldorf
being to get possession of the flying bridge,
and to carry that, with every boat and
barge that lay near, out of the reach of their

pursuers. Accordingly, after a halt of a few days, during which period Buonaparte with his staff and body-guard arrived, and a regiment of cavalry with some more infantry joined them, the whole moved off without having offered to the town the slightest molestation, and established themselves in a camp which had already been formed along the farther bank, and from which both they and their leaders hoped to guard effectually against the passage of the Rhine by the Allies.

END OF VOL. 1.

C. WHITING, BEAUFORT HOUSE, STRAND.

Lightning Source UK Ltd.
Milton Keynes UK
UKHW011025271218
334506UK00012B/740/P